The Billionaire's Mistaken Vow
An Age Gap Forced Proximity Romance
Chloe Horne

Copyright 2025 by Chloe Horne - All rights reserved.

In no way is it legal to reproduce, duplicate, or transmit any part of this document in either electronic means or in printed format. Recording of this publication is strictly prohibited and any storage of this document is not allowed unless with written permission from the publisher.

All rights reserved.

Respective authors own all copyrights not held by the publisher.

Contents

1. Chapter 1 — 1
2. Chapter 2 — 8
3. Chapter 3 — 16
4. Chapter 4 — 24
5. Chapter 5 — 35
6. Chapter 6 — 47
7. Chapter 7 — 54
8. Chapter 8 — 63
9. Chapter 9 — 73
10. Chapter 10 — 84
11. Chapter 11 — 92
12. Chapter 12 — 102
13. Chapter 13 — 112
14. Chapter 14 — 120
15. Chapter 15 — 127
16. Chapter 16 — 134
17. Chapter 17 — 142
18. Chapter 18 — 152

19.	Chapter 19	161
20.	Chapter 20	168
21.	Epilogue	176
Sneak Peak		183
with love and thanks		189

Chapter 1
Rachel

The Manhattan rain is trying to murder me, and honestly, I'm about to let it win.

I clutch the wrapped painting tighter against my chest as another gust of wind threatens to turn my umbrella inside out. Of course, today would be the day my boss decides I'm ready for a "major delivery" to some VIP collector's penthouse. Of course, it would be pouring like the apocalypse decided to take up residence in New York City.

"Shit, shit, shit," I mutter, dodging a puddle that looks deep enough to house a small ecosystem. My vintage emerald dress – the one that actually makes my curves look intentional instead of accidental – is getting soaked despite my best efforts. I probably should've worn something more professional, but this is literally the nicest thing I own that doesn't have paint stains.

The address my boss scrawled on a sticky note is barely legible now, thanks to the rain trying its damndest to wash away my last shred of confidence. Fifth Avenue. Penthouse. Some collector who apparently pays enough to keep our struggling gallery's lights on.

I squint up at the towering building, its glass facade reflecting the storm clouds like it's mocking my current drowned-rat aesthetic. The doorman – who looks like he costs more than my monthly rent – barely glances at me before waving me toward the elevators.

"Penthouse," I tell him, trying to sound like I belong here instead of like someone who clips coupons and considers ramen a food group.

He nods like I'm expected. Huh. Maybe this won't be a complete disaster after all.

The elevator ride to the top floor gives me enough time to practice my professional gallery assistant speech and attempt to fix my hair, which currently resembles what happens when you stick your finger in an electrical socket. By the time the doors slide open, I've managed to achieve "moderately presentable" instead of "victim of natural disaster."

The hallway screams money – the kind of quiet, understated wealth that doesn't need to shout about itself. I find the door and take a deep breath, adjusting my grip on the painting.

You've got this, Rachel. Just hand over the art, smile professionally, and try not to trip over your own feet.

I knock.

The door swings open, and my brain immediately flatlines.

Holy. Fucking. Hell.

Standing in the doorway is quite possibly the most gorgeous man I've ever seen outside of a magazine spread. And he's wearing nothing but a towel. A white towel that's slung dangerously low on narrow hips, defying both gravity and my ability to form coherent thoughts.

Water droplets trace lazy paths down his chest – and Jesus Christ, what a chest. Broad shoulders taper to a lean waist, every muscle defined like he was carved by someone who really, really enjoyed their job. His dark hair is damp and tousled, and when his ice-blue eyes meet mine, I swear I feel my ovaries spontaneously combust.

"Well," he says, his voice smooth as aged whiskey, "you're even more beautiful than I was told."

The painting slips from my nerveless fingers and hits the floor with a soft thud.

"I... what?" I stammer, my vocabulary apparently deciding to take an extended vacation.

His gaze travels down my body with obvious appreciation, lingering on the way my wet dress clings to my curves. "No need to be nervous, sweetheart. Come in."

He steps aside, gesturing toward what I assume is the living room, though all I can see is floor-to-ceiling windows showcasing a view of Central Park that probably costs more than I'll make in my lifetime.

"I should mention," he continues, that dangerous voice making my knees wobble, "you're early. I'll be a few minutes. Fix yourself a drink." His eyes flash with unmistakable heat. "I prefer to get to know one another before we leave for the opening."

My brain scrambles to process his words while my body betrays me with a flush of warmth that has nothing to do with embarrassment. Well, mostly nothing.

I stare at him, mouth agape like a fish drowning in air. This gorgeous, half-naked stranger thinks I'm here for... oh God. Oh no. OH NO.

"There's been a mistake," I finally manage, bending to retrieve the painting with shaking hands. "I'm here about the artwork. For the delivery? From the gallery?"

His expression shifts from desire to confusion, those piercing blue eyes narrowing slightly. "I didn't order any painting."

The way he says it makes my stomach drop. There's something darker in his tone now, something that makes me suddenly aware of how alone we are in this penthouse, how this man could probably snap me in half without breaking a sweat.

"But... the address..." I fumble with the soggy sticky note, holding it up like evidence. "My boss said you were expecting—"

"Your boss?" He steps closer, close enough that I can smell his expensive cologne mixing with soap and something indefinably masculine that makes my brain cells start abandoning ship. "And who exactly is your boss?"

Heat pools low in my belly despite the alarm bells going off in my head. This is bad. This is very, very bad. But the way he's looking at me – like he wants to devour me – is making parts of my anatomy wake up that have been hibernating since my last relationship ended in spectacular failure.

"I work for..." I start, then realize I probably shouldn't be giving personal information to strange men in towels who may or may not think I'm a prostitute.

He raises an eyebrow, a small smile playing at the corners of his mouth. "Cat got your tongue?"

The innuendo in his voice makes my nipples tighten against the wet fabric of my dress. From the way his gaze drops to my chest, he definitely notices.

"You're cold," he observes, his voice dropping to a near whisper. "Let me warm you up."

Before I can process what's happening, he reaches for the painting in my hands. The movement causes his towel to slip lower, revealing a tantalizing glimpse of the V-shaped muscles that disappear beneath the white terry cloth.

I can't help it – I stare. Because holy hell, this man's body should come with a warning label. Something like: Caution – May Cause Sudden Loss of Inhibitions and Questionable Life Choices.

"See something you like" he murmurs, his voice rough with amusement and something darker.

My cheeks flame, but I can't look away. "I... that is... your towel is..."

"Slipping?" He makes no move to adjust it. "Are you complaining?"

This is insane. I'm standing in a stranger's penthouse, soaking wet, probably committing some sort of breaking and entering by accident, while this sex god in a barely-there towel looks at me like I'm dessert and he's been on a diet for months.

And the worst part? I'm considering it.

"So," he says, stepping even closer until I can feel the heat radiating from his skin, "do you want to explain what you're really doing in my penthouse..." His towel slips another dangerous inch. "Or should I just close the door and find out for myself?"

The towel gives up entirely and drops.

I get approximately 0.3 seconds of full frontal glory before my survival instincts finally kick in.

"NOPE!" I shriek, spinning around so fast I nearly give myself whiplash. "Nope, nope, nope!"

I bolt for the door like my ass is on fire, the painting forgotten, my dignity left somewhere around the elevator shaft. My wet shoes have other plans though – they decide this is the perfect moment to betray me completely.

I slip.

Arms windmilling like a demented bird, I'm about to eat marble floor when strong hands catch me around the waist, pulling me back against a very warm, very naked chest.

"Easy there, sweetheart," he murmurs against my ear, his breath making me shiver. "Wouldn't want you to hurt yourself running away from me."

For one insane moment, I'm pressed against him, feeling every ridge of muscle, every inch of heated skin. My brain malfunctions so completely I think I might actually pass out.

"Holy fucking Christ on a cracker," I whisper.

His laughter rumbles through his chest and straight into my spine. "That's a new one."

I scramble out of his arms like he's made of molten lava, which honestly isn't far from the truth. "Sorry! Oh God, sorry! I just... your towel... and I slipped... and you're still naked!"

I don't look back. I can't look back. If I look back, I might do something incredibly stupid like offer to stay and discuss "art" while he's buck naked and looking like sin personified.

Instead, I sprint down the hallway, hit the elevator button approximately forty-seven times, and dive inside the moment the doors open.

"This is what I get for trying to be professional!" I yell at the closing elevator doors. "This is what I fucking get for wearing my good dress!"

The elevator descends in blessed silence while I try to pretend I'm not replaying the feeling of his hands on my waist or wondering what would've happened if I'd stayed.

Some mistakes, I tell myself firmly, are better left unmade.

Even if they come with abs that could make angels weep.

Chapter 2
Xander

I can't concentrate for shit, and it's all because of a curvy redhead who ran from my penthouse like I was the fucking devil himself.

"Xander, what are your thoughts on the quarterly projections?"

I blink, realizing I've been staring out the boardroom window for God knows how long while twelve executives wait for my input. Instead of analyzing profit margins, my brain keeps replaying the way her wet dress clung to every delicious curve, how her emerald eyes widened when she got an eyeful of me naked.

"The numbers look solid," I manage, though I couldn't tell you what numbers we're discussing if my life depended on it. "Continue with the implementation."

Gael shoots me a knowing smirk from across the mahogany table. The bastard can read me like a fucking book.

"Brilliant analysis as always," he drawls once the other board members file out. "Very thorough. I especially loved the part where you eye-fucked the window for twenty minutes."

"I was thinking," I mutter, loosening my tie.

"With your dick, apparently." He drops into the chair beside me, his expression far too amused. "Spill. Who's got Manhattan's most ruthless CEO twisted up like a pretzel?"

I consider lying, but Gael's been my best friend since Harvard. He'll figure it out eventually anyway. "Some woman delivered a painting to my place yesterday. Mix-up with the address."

"And?"

"And she saw me naked and bolted like I was about to sacrifice her to Satan."

Gael's grin could power half of Manhattan. "Holy shit. The Ice King finally meets a woman who isn't impressed by his massive—"

"Don't."

"—ego," he finishes with fake innocence. "What's she look like?"

Despite myself, my mind immediately conjures her image. Auburn hair that looked like liquid fire, skin pale as cream, and those fucking eyes. Green as sea glass and twice as mesmerizing. Then there were her tits—perfect handfuls straining against that vintage dress, nipples clearly visible through the wet fabric.

"She's..." I pause, searching for words that don't make me sound like a horny teenager. "Attractive."

"Christ, you've got it bad." Gael leans back, thoroughly entertained. "When's the last time you thought about a woman for more than five minutes after fucking her?"

Never. The answer is never, but I'm not giving him that ammunition. "Language, and I didn't fuck her."

"You should've kept her," he continues. "Locked the door, thrown her over your shoulder, caveman style. Women love that dominant shit."

"I think she thought I was expecting a prostitute."

Gael nearly chokes on his coffee. "What the fuck did you say to her?"

"I may have mentioned preferring to get to know each other before heading to the opening. Or other options."

"Jesus Christ, Xander. No wonder she ran. You basically propositioned a stranger."

The memory of her flushed cheeks and the way she stared at my body sends blood rushing south. She'd been nervous as hell, but there was something else in those green eyes. Heat.

Like drop towels and watch beautiful women flee.

"Forget about her," I tell myself as much as Gael. "It was a misunderstanding. End of story."

"Right," he says, not buying it for a second. "That's why you've mentioned her three times and keep adjusting your pants."

I flip him off and stride toward my office, determined to focus on actual work instead of some mystery woman who probably thinks I'm a perverted millionaire with boundary issues.

My assistant Maria buzzes me an hour later. "Mr. Ramsey? The painting delivered yesterday—our art appraiser says it's worth significantly more than the gallery quoted. It's apparently part of the Morrison collection you've been trying to acquire."

My blood turns to ice. "What gallery?"

"Meridian Arts. Your brother's place."

Julian. The painting came from Julian's gallery, which means...

"Get Julian on the phone. Now."

Two minutes later, my brother's voice crackles through the speaker. "Xander, what's wrong? You sound like someone pissed in your coffee."

"The painting delivered yesterday—who brought it?"

"Oh, that was Rachel. My new assistant. Sweet girl, bit scattered, but she's got an incredible eye for—"

"Rachel." The name feels like honey on my tongue.

"Yeah, Rachel Brooks. Why? Did she forget something? She seemed pretty flustered when she got back, kept muttering about towels and poor life choices."

Towels. Christ.

"She'll be at tonight's gala, won't she?" I ask, trying to sound casual.

"Of course. Why?" Julian's voice turns suspicious. "Xander, please tell me you're not planning to—"

I hang up before he can finish that sentence.

Maria appears in my doorway holding a tablet. "You wanted research on Rachel Brooks?"

Twenty minutes later, I know everything there is to know about the woman who's been haunting my thoughts. Foster care kid who aged out of the system at eighteen. Full scholarship to Parsons, graduated with honors while working three jobs. Lives in a studio apartment in Queens, takes the subway everywhere, clips coupons like it's an Olympic sport.

No trust fund. No wealthy parents. No ulterior motives.

She's nothing like the women who usually throw themselves at me—polished socialites who calculate every smile and see dollar signs when they look in my direction. Rachel Brooks is real. Authentic. And based on her financial situation, probably struggling to make rent.

The thought of her worrying about money while I have more than I could spend in ten lifetimes makes something twist in my chest.

By five PM, I'm at my private gym, attacking the punching bag like it owes me money. Sweat drips down my face as I imagine seeing her again tonight. Will she wear another vintage dress that hugs her curves like a second skin? Will she remember the way I looked at her, the heat that crackled between us before my towel hit the floor?

"Damn, man," calls Tony, my trainer, from across the room. "What'd that bag ever do to you?"

"Just working off some energy," I grunt, landing another brutal combination.

"Uh-huh. This got anything to do with a woman?"

THE BILLIONAIRE'S MISTAKEN VOW

I pause mid-swing. "What makes you say that?"

"Twenty years of training rich assholes, and I've never seen you this wound up. Someone's gotten under the Ice King's skin."

The Ice King. That's what they call me in the business world—ruthless, controlled, emotionally unavailable. But yesterday, when Rachel looked at my body with frank feminine appreciation, I'd felt anything but cold.

I'd felt like I was burning alive.

"She's going to be at some charity thing tonight," I admit, wrapping my hands.

"And you're planning to sweep her off her feet with your devastating charm and sparkling personality?"

"Something like that."

Tony snorts. "Good luck, Champ. Try not to terrify her into therapy."

Three hours later, I'm standing in the ballroom of the Plaza Hotel, scanning the crowd for auburn hair and green eyes. The annual Meridian Arts masquerade gala is in full swing—Manhattan's elite hiding behind elaborate masks while pretending to care about struggling artists.

I spot Julian near the bar, looking uncharacteristically tense. Something's wrong.

"Thank God you're here," he says when I approach. "We have a problem. Graham Whitfield just called—he's backing out of the Morrison collection purchase. Something about liquid assets and market volatility."

My blood chills. "How much was he supposed to invest?"

"Two point five million." Julian runs a hand through his hair. "Without that sale, I can't make payroll next month. I'll have to let people go."

"Don't do anything rash," I tell him, my mind already calculating solutions. "There are other collectors—"

"Who? You know how niche this market is. Whitfield was our best shot."

"How long before you have to make the cuts?" I ask, though my voice sounds distant to my own ears.

"End of the week." Julian sighs heavily. "I'm going to have to start with Rachel. She's the newest hire, part-time, and frankly, I can't afford to keep someone who's still learning the ropes when I need experienced staff to handle the crisis."

The words hit me like a sledgehammer to the chest. My blood turns to ice, and for a moment, I can't breathe. Rachel will lose her job. The woman who fled my penthouse in a panic, who looked at me with those gorgeous green eyes full of fire and vulnerability, will be unemployed by Friday.

She probably already struggles to pay rent in that tiny Queens apartment. Probably eats ramen more nights than she'd admit. And now she'll lose the one steady income keeping her afloat.

Something primal and protective claws at my chest, but I keep my expression neutral. Can't let Julian see how much this affects me.

"The art market will bounce back," I manage, my voice carefully controlled.

"Maybe. But I can't wait for maybe when I've got bills due now." Julian runs a hand through his hair. "Rachel's sweet, and she's got incredible instincts about art, but I have to be practical. She'll understand."

No, she fucking won't.

"There has to be another solution," I say, scanning the crowd of potential buyers while my mind races. "What about private collectors? The Hendersons have been looking for—"

"Already exhausted those options. Everyone's spooked about liquidity right now." Julian's voice drops with resignation. "Look, I hate this as much as you do, but I don't have a choice. I'll break the news to her gently, help her find something else if I can."

The thought of her face when she gets fired, the way her shoulders will slump with defeat, makes me want to demolish something with my bare hands. But I can't show that. Can't let Julian know that some woman I barely know has gotten under my skin so completely.

"Xander?" Julian waves a hand in front of my face. "Holy fucking hell, are you even listening to me?"

Chapter 3
Rachel

This dress is going to be the death of me.

Christina's borrowed black cocktail number clings to my curves like liquid sin, and these heels are basically medieval torture devices disguised as footwear. I wobble slightly as I navigate through Manhattan's glittering elite, balancing a champagne tray while trying not to face-plant into some billionaire's wife.

"You look incredible," Peyton had declared after attacking my face with enough makeup to open a Sephora. The smoky eyes she created make me look like someone completely different—someone who belongs at charity galas instead of clipping coupons at the grocery store.

"Remember," Christina whispered before shoving me into the Plaza's ballroom, "circulate, smile, and mention the Morrison collection to anyone wearing more than your monthly rent."

Right. Simple enough. Except I feel like an imposter wearing a borrowed life, and these Manhattan socialites can probably smell my thrift store origins from across the room.

"Champagne?" I offer to a woman dripping in diamonds, plastering on my most professional smile.

THE BILLIONAIRE'S MISTAKEN VOW 17

She barely glances at me before plucking a glass from my tray. "Lovely, dear."

I'm invisible here. Just another worker bee serving the queen bees, and honestly? That's perfectly fine by me. The last thing I need is attention from rich men who think I'm available for purchase.

A shiver runs down my spine as I remember yesterday's towel incident. Those ice-blue eyes, that perfectly sculpted chest, the way his voice dropped to pure sin when he—

"Fucking focus, Rachel," I mutter under my breath, nearly colliding with a server carrying canapés.

That's when I see him.

My breath catches in my throat as my eyes lock onto a tall figure across the room. Even with an elegant black mask covering half his face, I'd recognize those broad shoulders anywhere. That commanding presence that makes everyone else fade into background noise.

Holy shit on a cracker. It's him. Towel Guy is here, looking like every woman's fantasy in a perfectly tailored tuxedo that probably costs more than my yearly rent.

I duck behind a marble pillar, heart hammering against my ribs like it's trying to escape. Maybe he won't notice me. Maybe I can just hide behind decorative architecture until this nightmare ends.

Thank God for small mercies—he doesn't seem to recognize me. The mask, the makeup, the dress transformation worked. Relief floods through me so hard I nearly drop my champagne tray.

"Rachel!" Julian's voice cuts through my panic. "There you are."

I spin around, praying Towel Guy doesn't hear my name. "Julian! Hi! How's the... uh... gala-ing going?"

His expression makes my stomach plummet. "We need to talk. Privately."

Shit. That tone never means anything good.

He leads me to a quiet alcove near the windows, his face grim. "Graham Whitfield just called. He's pulling out of the Morrison collection purchase."

The words hit me like a sledgehammer. "What? But that's... that's our biggest sale this quarter."

"Two point five million down the drain." Julian runs his hands through his hair, destroying his usually perfect styling. "Without that money, I can't make payroll next month."

My champagne tray trembles in my hands. "What does that mean?"

"It means I have to make cuts. Starting with..." He pauses, and I already know what's coming. "I'm sorry, Rachel. You're the newest hire, part-time, and with the showcase for emerging artists now in jeopardy—"

"You're firing me." The words taste like ash in my mouth.

"I don't have a choice. The gallery's bleeding money, and I need experienced staff to navigate this crisis."

I nod numbly, trying to process the information. No job means no rent. No rent means back to sleeping on Peyton's couch, assuming she can even afford to keep her place. No steady income means my art supplies become luxuries I can't afford.

"I understand," I manage, proud that my voice doesn't crack. "When?"

"End of the week. I'll give you the best recommendation possible, help you find something else—"

"It's fine," I interrupt, forcing a smile. "These things happen, right? Art market's unpredictable."

Julian looks miserable. "Rachel—"

"I should get back to work. While I still have a job to do."

I escape to the terrace before he can say anything else, gulping the cool night air like a drowning woman. The city sparkles below, all those lights representing dreams and opportunities that feel impossibly far away.

"Rough night?"

I nearly jump out of my skin at the smooth, familiar voice. Towel Guy approaches with two champagne flutes, his black mask making his blue eyes even more intense. Up close, he's devastating—the mask accentuates his sharp jawline, and the tuxedo transforms him from naked temptation into sophisticated sin.

My heart pounds, but his expression shows no recognition. The mask is working. Thank you, sweet baby Jesus and all the saints.

"You could say that," I reply, accepting the champagne because my hands need something to do other than shake.

"Beautiful view." He moves to stand beside me at the railing, close enough that I catch his expensive cologne. "Though I imagine the company matters more than the scenery."

"Are you hitting on me?" The words slip out before I can stop them.

His laugh is rich and warm. "Direct. I like that. Most women at these events speak in riddles and hidden meanings."

"Maybe because most women here are afraid of saying the wrong thing to the wrong billionaire."

"And you're not?"

I take a sip of champagne, feeling oddly bold behind my mask. "I'm working class, remember? We tend to speak our minds."

"Working class?" His eyebrow arches. "At a charity gala?"

"Serving the champagne, not drinking it. Well, except for right now." I gesture with my glass. "Thanks for this, by the way."

"My pleasure." His voice drops slightly. "What do you do when you're not serving drinks to Manhattan's elite?"

Great, he doesn't recognize me, so maybe I can have a normal conversation with an insanely attractive man for once in my pathetic dating life.

"I work at an art gallery. Assistant level, nothing glamorous."

THE BILLIONAIRE'S MISTAKEN VOW

"Art's never nothing glamorous. What kind of pieces does your gallery feature?"

"Contemporary mostly. Some established artists, some emerging talent trying to make it in the big, bad city."

"And are you? Trying to make it, I mean."

Heat creeps up my neck. "Maybe. I paint when I'm not working my ass off to pay rent."

"What do you paint?"

"Abstract stuff. Emotions, experiences, feelings that don't have words." I'm rambling again, but something about his attention makes me want to keep talking. "It's probably pretentious bullshit to most people."

"Art should make you feel something. If it doesn't, what's the point?" He turns to study my profile. "Do you show your work anywhere?"

"God, no. I'm nowhere near ready for that kind of exposure." The irony of discussing exposure with a man who's seen me completely flustered isn't lost on me. "What about you? What do you do when you're not attending fancy charity events?"

"Business. Investments. The usual boring rich guy stuff."

"Boring rich guy stuff that affords you thousand-dollar tuxedos?"

His grin is dangerous. "You noticed the tuxedo?"

"Hard not to. It fits you like it was sewn directly onto your body."

"Are you flirting with me now?"

My cheeks flame. "Maybe. Is it working?"

"Definitely." His voice goes rough around the edges. "Though I have to warn you, I'm not great at small talk."

"What are you great at?"

His eyes darken as they travel over my face, lingering on my lips.

"Other things," he says finally.

"Such as?"

"Getting what I want."

"And what is it you want?"

"Right now?" He steps closer, close enough that I can feel the heat radiating from his body. "To know your name."

Panic flutters in my chest. Names lead to recognition, and recognition leads to awkward explanations about yesterday's towel incident.

"Names are overrated," I manage. "Mystery is more fun."

"Mystery." He considers this, his gaze intense. "I can work with mystery."

The clock tower chimes eleven-thirty, and my heart jumps. Half an hour until midnight, when everyone removes their masks. Half an hour to enjoy this fantasy.

Before I can say anything else, he's stepping closer again, close enough that I have to tilt my head back to maintain eye contact.

"Dance with me," he says, not really a question.

"I told you, I'm working—"

"The night's almost over. One dance."

"I don't really know how to dance. Not ballroom stuff, anyway."

"I'll lead." His hand extends toward me. "Trust me."

Those two words shouldn't make my entire nervous system light up like a Christmas tree, but here we are.

I'm reaching for his hand when I feel it—my mask slipping. The ribbon must have loosened during our conversation, and gravity is working against me in the worst possible way.

"Oh fuck," I whisper, reaching up to catch it.

But it's too late. The black silk falls away, leaving me completely exposed under his intense stare.

I'm staring into the face of yesterday's naked stranger, and this time there's nowhere left to run.

Chapter 4
Xander

Holy fucking hell.

The mask falls from her fingers like silk surrendering to gravity, and I'm staring into those stunning emerald eyes I've been dreaming about for twenty-four goddamn hours. The woman who's about to lose her job because my brother can't keep his business afloat.

"Shit," she whispers, her face flushing that gorgeous pink that makes me want to taste every inch of her skin.

"Language," I murmur automatically, though my brain is currently occupied with more pressing matters. Like how her borrowed dress hugs her curves so perfectly it should be illegal. Like how I want to press her against the nearest wall and find out if she tastes as sweet as she looks.

"You," she breathes, taking a step backward.

"Me," I confirm, moving closer to compensate for her retreat. "Though I have to say, you clean up nicely. Much better than the drowned rat look you were sporting yesterday."

Her mouth drops open in indignation. "Excuse me? I was soaking wet from—"

"The rain. Yes, I remember." My gaze drops to her lips, full and glossy with whatever lipstick her friend applied. "Among other things."

The way her breath hitches makes my dick strain against my tuxedo pants. Christ, this woman affects me like no one ever has.

"I should go," she says, but doesn't move. Just stands there staring at me like I'm a car accident she can't look away from.

"Should you?" I step closer, close enough to smell her vanilla perfume mixing with nervous sweat. "Because from where I'm standing, it looks like you want to stay."

"You're delusional."

"Am I?" I tilt my head, studying the way her pupils are dilated despite the terrace lighting. "Your body language suggests otherwise."

"My body language—" She sputters, crossing her arms over her chest, which only pushes her breasts higher in that sinful dress. "You arrogant prick."

"Now who's using inappropriate language?" I can't help but smile at her fire. Most women either throw themselves at me or cower in intimidation. Rachel does neither. She stands her ground and calls me names, and it's the most attractive thing I've ever witnessed.

"This is insane," she mutters, running shaking hands through her auburn hair. "I'm talking to a stranger who saw me practically hyperventilate over his naked body."

"Technically, we've been talking for twenty minutes. That makes us acquaintances at least."

"Acquaintances don't usually involve nudity and towel incidents."

"You'd be surprised." The way she blushes makes me want to discover what other innocent comments can make her face turn that delicious shade of pink. "Besides, you seemed to enjoy the view yesterday."

"I did not—" She catches herself, those green eyes narrowing. "You're enjoying this. My mortification is entertainment for you."

"Your mortification is many things, but entertainment isn't one of them." I move closer, backing her against the stone railing. "Want to know what it actually is?"

"No," she says quickly. Too quickly.

"It's fucking intoxicating," I continue, ignoring her protest. "The way you blush, the way you can't quite meet my eyes when you're remembering what I look like naked. The way you're trying so hard to pretend you don't want me to kiss you right now."

Her breath catches audibly. "I don't—"

"Liar." I reach up to cup her face, thumb brushing across her lower lip. "Your pulse is racing. I can see it in your throat."

"Maybe because you're scaring me."

"Maybe. Or maybe because you're wondering what would happen if you stopped running from me."

She stares up at me with those expressive eyes, her lips parted slightly like an invitation I'm dying to accept. The sounds of the party fade into background noise as everything narrows to this moment, this woman, this need clawing at my chest.

"You don't know anything about me," she whispers.

"I know you work for Julian. I know you grew up in foster care and graduated with honors while working three jobs. I know you live in Queens and take the subway and probably eat noodle based cuisine more often than you'd admit."

Her eyes widen. "You had me investigated?"

"I had you researched. There's a difference."

"That's so much worse!" She tries to step away, but the railing prevents her escape. "What kind of psychopath—"

"The kind who can't stop thinking about a woman who ran from his penthouse in a panic," I interrupt, my voice rougher than intended. "The kind who's been hard for twenty-four hours straight because he can't forget the way she looked at his body."

"Jesus Christ," she breathes.

"Dance with me."

"What?"

"You heard me. One dance before you inevitably flee again."

"I'm working—"

"Fuck the job." The vehemence in my voice surprises us both. "Dance with me, Rachel."

She studies my face for a long moment, and I can practically see the internal debate raging behind those gorgeous eyes. Finally, impossibly, she nods.

I lead her to a secluded corner of the terrace where the music drifts from the ballroom speakers. Other couples sway nearby, but they might as well be on another planet for all the attention I'm paying them.

The moment I pull her into my arms, everything else ceases to exist.

Her curves fit against my body like she was custom-made for me. Her vanilla scent fills my nostrils, and the way she trembles slightly—whether from nervousness or desire—makes my protective instincts flare alongside the lust threatening to consume me.

"Relax," I murmur against her ear, feeling her shiver. "I promised to lead, remember?"

"I don't know how to do this," she admits, her voice barely audible over the music.

"Do what? Dance?"

"Any of this. I don't belong in your world."

I pull back to look at her face, studying the uncertainty written across her delicate features.

"My world is pretty fucking empty," I tell her honestly. "Maybe I need someone who doesn't belong in it."

"You don't mean that."

"Don't I?" My hand finds the small of her back, pressing her closer until there's no space between us. "You want to know what I think?"

"Not particularly," she lies.

"I think you're exactly where you belong. Right here, in my arms, driving me completely out of my goddamn mind."

Her breathing becomes shallow, and I can feel her heart hammering against her ribs. "This is crazy."

"The best things usually are." I spin her slowly, watching the way her dress flares around her legs. "Tell me about your art."

The subject change catches her off guard. "What?"

"Your painting. What emotions are you trying to capture?"

She considers the question seriously, her guard dropping slightly. "Longing, mostly. The feeling of wanting something you can't have. The ache of almost belonging somewhere but not quite."

"And do you? Almost belong somewhere?"

"I thought I did. At the gallery. But..." She trails off, pain flashing across her face.

"But what?"

"Nothing. It doesn't matter."

But it does matter. It matters because in a few hours, she'll be unemployed and struggling, and the thought makes me want to burn down half of Manhattan to keep her safe.

I don't know why but I don't tell her that the Julian who is going to fire her is my brother.

The music slows, and I pull her closer until we're barely moving, just swaying together in the shadows. Her hands rest on my chest, and I can feel the heat of her palms through my shirt.

"Why did you run yesterday?" I ask quietly.

"Because you were naked and gorgeous and I was having very inappropriate thoughts about a complete stranger."

"What kind of inappropriate thoughts?"

Her cheeks flame. "The kind that would get me in trouble."

"What if I want you to get in trouble?"

She looks up at me then, those green eyes dark with something that makes my blood catch fire. "What are you suggesting?"

"That we find somewhere more private."

"Private?" she whispers, and Christ, I've never heard anything more beautiful in my entire life.

I can't take it anymore. The need to taste her, to feel her respond to me, overwhelms every rational thought I've ever had.

"Rachel," I murmur, cupping her face with both hands. "I'm going to kiss you now. If you don't want that, tell me to stop."

Instead of protesting, she rises on her toes to meet me halfway.

Our lips crash together like months of attraction compressed into one perfect, desperate moment. She tastes like champagne and something indefinably sweet, and when she opens her mouth to let me deeper, I nearly lose every thought ever in my head.

Her hands fist in my shirt as I back her toward a shadowed alcove, hidden from the other guests by decorative columns and trailing ivy. The distant sounds of the party fade to nothing as I press her against the stone wall, my body caging her in.

"Fuck," I breathe against her lips. "You taste even better than I imagined."

"You imagined?" she gasps between kisses.

"All fucking night. All day. I haven't been able to think about anything else."

My hands roam her curves, relearning the shape of her through expensive fabric. She arches into my touch, soft moans escaping her throat that drive me absolutely wild.

She whimpers when I kiss down her neck, finding that sensitive spot that makes her knees buckle. "We shouldn't—"

"Why not?" I lift her slightly, her legs wrapping around my waist instinctively. "Because you think I'm out of your league? Because you're afraid of how good this could be?"

"All of the above," she admits, but her body betrays her words as she grinds against me desperately.

I can feel her heat through our clothes, and it takes every ounce of self-control I possess not to take her right here against this wall.

"How does this feel?" I murmur, my hand sliding up her thigh beneath the silk dress.

Her face flushes deeper. "Like I'm losing my mind."

"Good. That makes two of us." My fingers find the edge of her panties, and she gasps sharply.

Instead of stopping me, she pulls my head down for another desperate kiss. I take that as permission to slide my hand inside her dress, finding her slick and ready for me.

"Christ, you're so wet," I groan against her mouth.

"Don't say things like that," she pants, but her hips buck against my hand.

"Why not? It's true." I stroke her slowly, watching her eyes flutter closed. "You like it when I touch you like this."

"Yes," she admits breathlessly. "God, yes."

I slip one finger inside her panties, finding her clit. She cries out, her nails digging into my shoulders as I start to circle the sensitive bundle of nerves.

Please—"

"Please what, sweetheart?"

"I don't know. More. Something. I can't think straight."

My cock strains against my pants, hard as steel from watching her come apart in my arms. I push her panties aside completely, needing better access to drive her wild.

"Look at me," I command, and her eyes snap open, dark with desire. "I want to watch your face when you come."

"We can't—someone might see—"

"Let them," I growl, adding pressure to my movements. "Let them see how beautiful you look falling apart for me."

Her breathing becomes ragged, and I can feel her getting closer to the edge. The way she responds to my touch, the little sounds she makes, the way her body trembles—it's the most erotic thing I've ever experienced.

I'm going to—"

"That's it, baby. Come for me."

Just as she's about to shatter completely, voices drift closer to our hidden alcove. Reality crashes back like cold water, and we break apart, breathing heavily and staring at each other with shock at the intensity between us.

"Fuck," I mutter, stepping back to give her space while she straightens her dress with shaking hands.

"That was..." She trails off, unable to finish the sentence.

"Incredible," I supply, reaching out to smooth her hair. "And completely insane."

She fixes my bow tie with gentle fingers, the intimate gesture feeling more significant than it should. For a moment, we just stand there, lost in each other's eyes.

Then she runs.

Again.

"Rachel, wait—" But she's already disappearing into the crowd, leaving me alone and harder than I've ever been in my entire life.

I lean against the wall, trying to get my breathing under control. Twenty-four hours ago, I didn't even know her name. Now I'm completely obsessed with a woman who works for my brother and has no idea the effect she has on me.

The thought of seeing her tomorrow in a professional context after what just happened makes my blood burn with anticipation. This isn't over. Not by a long shot.

If anything, it's just beginning.

Chapter 5
Rachel

I arrive at the gallery at seven-thirty in the morning, clutching my third cup of coffee like it's the only thing standing between me and a complete mental breakdown.

Which, honestly, it might be.

My reflection in the gallery's front windows looks like I've been hit by a tornado. My hair refuses to cooperate despite twenty minutes of aggressive brushing, and no amount of concealer can hide the dark circles under my eyes from a sleepless night spent replaying every single second of what happened on that terrace.

Towel Guy's hands between my thighs. Towel Guy's mouth on mine. Towel Guy making me feel like I was going to spontaneously combust from pure want.

"Fuck my entire life," I mutter, fumbling with my keys.

The gallery feels different this morning. I flip on the lights and immediately bustle toward my desk, desperate for the familiar routine of work to erase the memory of ice-blue eyes and the way his voice dropped to pure sin when he called me beautiful.

My phone buzzes with a text from Peyton: *Spill everything RIGHT NOW or I'm staging an intervention.*

Before I can even consider ignoring her, my phone starts ringing.

"You better start talking, Brooks," Peyton's voice crackles through the speaker. "Because you left that gala looking like you'd been thoroughly debauched, and I need details immediately."

"I have no idea what you're talking about," I lie, sorting through yesterday's invoices with shaking hands.

"Bullshit. Your hair was fucked up, your lipstick was gone, and you had that post-makeout glow that could power Times Square." She pauses dramatically. "So who was he? Rich? Gorgeous? Packing impressive equipment?"

"Peyton!"

"What? These are important questions! Did you at least get his number, or are we dealing with a Cinderella situation where you fled at midnight like a sexually frustrated pumpkin?"

I drop my head into my hands. "It's complicated."

"Complicated how? Did he turn out to be married? Gay? Related to you?"

"Worse. He's..." I struggle to find words that don't make me sound completely insane. "He's intimidating. Rich. Probably thinks I'm an idiot who doesn't know how to act around sophisticated people."

"Or he thinks you're amazing and wants to worship your body like the temple it is." Peyton's voice turns serious. "Rach, when's the last time you let yourself feel good about attracting someone? Like, genuinely good instead of immediately assuming you're not worthy?"

"That's not—"

"It absolutely is what you're doing. You met someone who made you feel desired, and now you're spiraling because you can't believe someone might actually want you for you."

Before I can argue, she continues. "Did you sleep with him?"

"No! Jesus, what kind of person do you think I am?"

"The kind who deserves mind-blowing orgasms with hot strangers. So, what happened? Heavy petting? Oral? Please tell me you at least got some action after the dating drought you've been enduring."

My cheeks flame. "We... kissed. And he... touched me. A little."

"How little? Like, over-the-clothes touching or under-the-panties touching?"

"Peyton!"

"That's under-the-panties touching! Holy shit, Rach! You let some gorgeous stranger finger you at a charity gala? I'm so fucking proud right now."

"We didn't... I mean, we were interrupted before anything really happened."

"Define 'really happened.'"

"Before I could... you know. Finish."

Peyton's silence stretches for exactly three seconds before she explodes. "That bastard left you hanging? What kind of monster blue-balls a woman at a fancy party? You need to find this man and demand he complete what he started. It's a matter of principle."

"I can't just track down random men and demand sexual satisfaction!"

"Why the hell not? You think guys don't do that exact thing? Find him, Rach. Seduce him. Get yourself properly laid for once in your goddamn life. It's exactly that simple. You're twenty-six years old and gorgeous, and you've been celibate for so long I'm surprised your vagina hasn't sealed itself shut from disuse."

"That's not how vaginas work!"

"My point stands. Find mystery man. Fuck his brains out. Report back with explicit details."

Before I can explain why that's impossible, the gallery door chimes. Julian walks in looking like he hasn't slept in weeks, his usually perfect hair sticking up at odd angles.

"I have to go," I tell Peyton quickly. "Julian's here."

"This conversation isn't over! I want names, positions, and a detailed analysis of his oral technique!"

I hang up, my face burning. "Morning, Julian. You're here early."

"Crisis mode," he mutters, heading straight for the coffee machine. "Xander's coming by this morning to discuss a potential investment, and I'm terrified I'm going to say something stupid and blow our only chance at survival."

My stomach drops like I've been pushed off a cliff. "Xander?"

"My brother. Xander Ramsey. I mentioned him before—billionaire, terrifying business instincts, probably our last hope for keeping this place afloat."

The coffee mug slips from my suddenly nerveless fingers, shattering against the floor in an explosion of ceramic and caffeine.

"Shit! Sorry!" I dive for the paper towels, my mind reeling. "Your brother Xander? As in... Xander Ramsey?"

"Yeah. Why?" Julian studies my face with growing concern. "Do you know him?"

"No! I mean, not really. Just... heard the name around. Business circles. Rich guy stuff." I'm babbling while frantically mopping up coffee, trying to process this information. "He's your brother?"

"Half-brother, technically. Different mothers, same workaholic father who taught us both that money matters more than relationships." Julian's expression turns grim.

I nod mutely, my throat tight with humiliation. How could I have been so stupid?

"Rachel? You okay? You look kind of pale."

"Fine," I manage. "Just tired. Long night."

"Right. Well, he'll be here in an hour, so let's get organized. The Morrison collection paperwork needs to be ready, and I want the emerging artists showcase materials prepared in case he's interested in supporting local talent."

I spend the next forty-five minutes throwing myself into work, organizing portfolios and contracts with manic energy. If I stay busy enough, maybe I can convince myself that last night was just a weird dream instead of the most erotic experience of my pathetic life.

When I'm arranging my own pieces for the emerging artists showcase—three abstract paintings that suddenly look amateurish and embarrassing—Christina arrives with two cups of expensive coffee and a knowing grin.

"Well, well, well," she says, settling gracefully into the chair across from my desk. "Someone had an interesting evening."

"I have no idea what you mean," I lie, not looking up from my paintings.

"The mysterious glow, the slightly rumpled appearance, the way you keep touching your lips like you're remembering something delicious..." Christina's eyes sparkle with mischief. "Who was he? Anyone I know?"

"There was no 'he.'"

"Please. I saw you disappear onto the terrace with someone tall, dark, and expensive-looking. Then you vanished completely, and your friend Peyton spent twenty minutes looking for you before giving up."

My cheeks burn. "It was nothing. Just a dance."

"Honey, I've seen 'just a dance,' and that wasn't it. You looked thoroughly kissed when you finally resurfaced." Christina leans forward conspiratorially. "Was it good? Please tell me it was good, because the dating scene in this city is absolutely brutal."

"Can we please not discuss my nonexistent love life?"

"Nonexistent? So, something did happen!" Christina claps her hands together. "I knew it! You have that post-makeout energy that's impossible to fake. Well, get ready for a big day. I heard Julian say his brother Xander is visiting. He's one of the biggest donors. Though he usually keeps to himself, all business and intimidation."

The gallery door chimes, and my heart stops completely.

Because walking through the entrance, looking devastatingly handsome in a charcoal suit, is Xander fucking Towel Guy.

Our eyes meet across the gallery space, and the heat between us is immediate and overwhelming. His gaze travels over my body, lingering on my mouth like he's remembering exactly how I tasted.

"Holy shit," Christina breathes. "Is that...?"

But I can't answer because Julian is emerging from his office, completely oblivious to the sexual tension crackling through the air like lightning.

"Xander! Right on time. Thanks for coming."

Xander's eyes never leave mine as he extends his hand to his brother. "My pleasure, Julian. I'm very interested in seeing what you've been working on."

His voice, smooth as aged whiskey, sends shivers down my spine. The same voice that whispered dirty things against my ear while his fingers drove me wild.

I'm so completely fucked.

"Rachel," Julian calls, completely oblivious to my internal meltdown. "Come meet my brother. Xander, this is Rachel Brooks, our part-time assistant I was telling you about."

Xander steps forward, extending his hand with a slight smile that doesn't reach his eyes. "Ms. Brooks. A pleasure."

When our fingers touch, electricity shoots straight through my nervous system. His thumb brushes across my knuckles in a gesture that appears innocent but feels incredibly intimate.

"Mr. Ramsey," I manage, proud that my voice doesn't crack. "Welcome to Meridian Arts."

"Thank you." His grip lingers a fraction too long before he releases my hand. "Julian tells me you have an excellent eye for emerging talent."

"I... yes. I try to stay current with local artists and contemporary trends."

"Fascinating." His blue eyes hold mine captive. "I'd love to hear your thoughts on the current market sometime."

Christina clears her throat loudly. "I should let you get to your meeting. Rachel, don't forget about the showcase preparations."

She practically floats out of the gallery, shooting me a look that clearly says *we're discussing this later*.

"Right," Julian says, clapping his hands together. "Let's head to my office. We have a lot to cover."

THE BILLIONAIRE'S MISTAKEN VOW 43

As they walk toward the glass-walled office, Xander glances back at me, his gaze dropping to my mouth for just a moment. The memory of his lips on mine floods back in vivid detail, making my knees wobble.

I busy myself with filing, desperately trying to ignore the sound of their voices drifting through the thin walls. Xander's deep baritone carries clearly as he discusses investment strategies and market analysis with obvious expertise.

"The contemporary art market has shown remarkable resilience," he's saying. "Particularly pieces that combine emotional authenticity with technical skill."

"Exactly what we're trying to showcase," Julian responds. "The emerging artists exhibition could be our breakthrough event if we get the right backing."

"Tell me more about these local artists. What makes them worth investing in?"

My hands freeze on the filing cabinet. Through the glass partition, I can see Xander leaning back in his chair, completely at ease in the business environment that intimidates most people.

"We have several promising pieces," Julian continues. "Contemporary abstracts, some stunning realistic portraits, a few mixed-media installations that push boundaries..."

"Any particular artist catching your attention?"

"Actually, yes. Rachel's work is exceptional. Raw emotion combined with sophisticated technique. She's been hiding her talent, but I think she's ready for serious exposure."

My heart stops. Through the glass, I watch Xander's expression sharpen with interest.

"Really? I'd be very interested in seeing her portfolio."

"I'll have her prepare everything for review. In fact..." Julian turns toward the main gallery space. "Rachel! Could you bring your showcase pieces to the office? Xander would like to take a look."

Fuck. Fuck, fuck, fuck.

There's no escape. I gather my three paintings with trembling hands, acutely aware that I'm about to present my most personal work to the man who had his fingers inside my panties less than twelve hours ago.

When I enter the office, Xander stands immediately—perfect manners that probably came from some expensive boarding school. His presence fills the small space completely, making it hard to breathe.

"Please, have a seat," he says, gesturing to the chair across from his.

I perch on the edge, clutching my paintings like shields. "These are just preliminary pieces. Nothing too sophisticated or..."

"May I?" He reaches for the first canvas, his fingers brushing mine as he takes it.

The contact sends heat shooting straight between my legs. His eyes meet mine for a split second, and I swear I see the same memory flashing behind his blue gaze.

He examines my painting with genuine attention—a swirling mass of blues and grays that I created during a particularly lonely night last month. Colors bleeding into each other like tears, harsh lines softened by gentle curves.

"This is remarkable," he says quietly. "There's so much longing in the brushstrokes. So much... hunger."

The way he says 'hunger' makes my nipples tighten against my bra. Julian, thankfully, seems oblivious to the sexual undercurrent crackling between us.

"Rachel's always been modest about her talent," Julian says proudly. "But I think she's ready for a major showcase. With the right financial backing, we could really launch her career."

Xander moves to the second painting—bolder reds and oranges that represent passion and desire. Colors I was too afraid to explore until recently.

"And this one?" His voice drops slightly. "What inspired this piece?"

I can barely form words. "It's about... awakening. Discovering parts of yourself you didn't know existed."

His gaze burns into mine. "Powerful theme. Very... evocative."

The third painting makes my cheeks flame with embarrassment. It's the most recent one, created just two days ago after a particularly vivid dream about ice-blue eyes and skilled hands. Deep purples and midnight blues swirling around a center of pure golden light.

"This is your most recent work?" Xander asks, studying it intently.

"Yes. It's... it represents yearning. For connection. For someone who sees the real you beneath all the barriers you've built."

The silence stretches between us, thick with unspoken recognition. Julian shifts in his chair, clearly sensing something but not sure what.

"These are extraordinary, Rachel," Xander says finally. "Julian's right—you're ready for serious exposure. I'd like to discuss featuring your work in my private collection showcase next month."

My mouth falls open. "Your private collection?"

"I host an annual event for emerging artists. Invitation only, serious collectors, significant sales potential." His eyes never leave mine. "Would you be interested in participating?"

"I... yes. Of course. That would be incredible."

This is either the best thing that's ever happened to me, or I'm about to make the biggest mistake of my life.

Probably both.

Chapter 6
Xander

Watching Rachel explain her artistic process is pure fucking torture.

She's gesticulating wildly as she describes her color theory, auburn hair catching the afternoon light streaming through Julian's office windows. Her vintage dress—forest green today, Christ help me—hugs every curve I memorized with my hands last night.

"The emotional resonance comes from layering transparent glazes," she's saying, completely absorbed in her subject. "Each layer represents a different aspect of the feeling I'm trying to capture."

I nod like I'm listening to her words instead of imagining peeling that dress off her gorgeous body and finding out if she tastes as sweet everywhere as she did on that terrace.

"Fascinating technique," I manage, adjusting my position to hide the hard-on that's been plaguing me since she walked into this office. "How do you achieve such depth in the darker sections?"

"Oh!" Her face lights up with genuine excitement. "I use a combination of burnt umber and Prussian blue, but the trick is applying it while the previous layer is still slightly tacky. Creates this incredible texture that—"

She stops mid-sentence, realizing she's been talking with her hands again. One delicate finger is pressed against her lower lip as she concentrates, and all I can think about is how those lips felt moving beneath mine.

"Sorry," she mumbles, tucking a strand of hair behind her ear. "I get carried away talking about paint."

"Don't apologize," I tell her, and mean it. "Passion is rare. Most people never find something that ignites them like this."

Her cheeks flush that delicious pink that makes me want to discover what other parts of her body turn that same shade when she's aroused.

"Xander," Julian interrupts, appearing in the doorway. "Gael's here to see you. Should I send him in?"

Fuck. The last thing I need is Gael's crude commentary when I'm barely maintaining professional composure around Rachel.

"Of course," I say, because refusing would raise questions I'm not ready to answer.

Gael saunters in wearing his trademark shit-eating grin, expensive suit wrinkled from whatever debauchery he engaged in last night. His eyes immediately lock onto Rachel, and I watch his expression shift into full predator mode.

"Well, well," he drawls, extending his hand. "You must be the mysterious gallery assistant."

Rachel's face goes scarlet. "I'm sorry?"

"Gael," I warn, my voice dropping to dangerous levels.

"What? I'm just making conversation." He turns back to Rachel, his grin widening. "I'm Gael Andrews, Xander's oldest friend and current voice of reason."

His gaze travels over Rachel's curves with obvious appreciation, and something primal claws at my chest. The urge to plant my fist in his face surprises me with its intensity.

"Ms. Brooks was showing me her portfolio," I say evenly. "Her work is exceptional."

"I bet it is," Gael murmurs, still eye-fucking her like she's dessert. "What kind of art do you create, honey?"

"Abstract expressionism, mostly," Rachel answers, her voice barely above a whisper. "Emotional landscapes, color studies..."

"Emotional landscapes," Gael repeats, his tone dripping innuendo. "Sounds fascinating. Very... intimate."

"Perhaps we could discuss the investment terms now," I interrupt before he can say something that makes me commit murder in my brother's office.

"Right, business first." Gael settles into the chair beside Rachel, close enough that she shifts uncomfortably. "Though I have to say, Xander rarely shows this much personal interest in his investments. Usually, he's all spreadsheets and profit margins."

"The art market requires more nuanced evaluation," I reply carefully.

"Does it? Or does the artist require more... hands-on assessment?"

I'm going to fucking kill him.

"Julian," I say, standing abruptly. "Let's finalize the numbers. Two point five million for the Morrison collection, plus an additional five hundred thousand for the emerging artists showcase."

Julian's mouth falls open. "Five hundred thousand?"

"Provided Ms. Brooks agrees to be featured as the headlining artist. Her work deserves serious exposure."

Rachel makes a small choking sound. "Headlining artist?"

"Your pieces have the emotional depth and technical skill to anchor the entire exhibition," I explain, keeping my voice professionally neutral despite the way she's staring at me like I've lost my mind. "With proper promotion and the right collectors in attendance, this could launch your career."

"But I'm not ready for that kind of attention. I'm nobody special, just—"

"You're extraordinary," I cut her off, the words coming out rougher than intended. "Your art speaks to something most people spend their entire lives searching for."

The silence that follows is deafening. Julian looks confused, Gael appears thoroughly entertained, and Rachel stares at me with those gorgeous green eyes wide with shock.

"Well," Gael says finally, "this just got interesting."

"I should go," Rachel mumbles, standing quickly and gathering her paintings. "Let you discuss business properly."

THE BILLIONAIRE'S MISTAKEN VOW 51

As she reaches for the largest canvas, I stand to help her, our hands brushing as we both grab the frame. The contact sends electricity shooting through my entire nervous system, making me freeze completely.

She's close enough that I can smell her vanilla perfume, see the rapid pulse fluttering in her throat. For one insane moment, I consider kissing her right here in front of my brother and best friend, consequences be damned.

"Thank you," she whispers, not pulling away.

"My pleasure," I murmur back, thumb brushing across her knuckles.

"Jesus Christ," Gael mutters under his breath.

Rachel jerks back like she's been burned, nearly dropping the painting in her haste to escape. "I'll just... put these away safely."

She bolts from the office, leaving me staring after her.

"Well, fuck me sideways," Gael says cheerfully. "The Ice King's got it bad."

"Shut up," I growl, dropping back into my chair.

"Xander," Julian says carefully, "is there something I should know about?"

"Just that your assistant is incredibly talented and deserves recognition for her work."

"Uh-huh." Julian doesn't look convinced. "Because for a minute there, it seemed like—"

"Like what?"

"Like you two were about to spontaneously combust from sexual tension," Gael supplies helpfully. "Which, by the way, was hot as hell to watch. She's gorgeous, by the way. Those tits alone could—"

"Finish that sentence and I'll break your jaw," I interrupt, my voice deadly calm.

Gael's grin widens. "There it is. The territorial caveman response."

I don't answer, which is answer enough.

Rachel reappears in the doorway, having composed herself enough to look professionally neutral again.

"Sorry to interrupt," she says, voice carefully controlled. "Julian, you wanted me to organize the client contact database before I leave today?"

"Actually," Julian says, glancing between us, "we were just discussing the exhibition timeline. Xander's investment means we can move forward with the showcase as planned for next month."

"Next month?" Rachel's voice cracks slightly.

"Which means," Julian continues, a slow smile spreading across his face, "you'll be working closely with Xander on the curatorial aspects. Daily meetings, portfolio development, collector presentations..."

My dick twitches at the thought of daily meetings with Rachel. Long, private sessions where we discuss her art and I slowly break down every wall she's built around herself.

"Daily meetings," she repeats faintly.

"Is that a problem?" I ask, keeping my expression neutral despite the predatory satisfaction coursing through my veins.

"No," she says quickly. "No problem at all."

Liar. She looks like she's about to pass out from panic.

"Excellent," Julian says, completely oblivious to the undercurrent of sexual tension threatening to suffocate us all. "Xander, why don't you and Rachel schedule your first session for tomorrow? My office is available all afternoon."

"Perfect," I say, never taking my eyes off her flushed face. "I'm very much looking forward to getting started."

Rachel's lips part slightly, and I swear I can hear her breath catch.

This is either going to be the best month of my life, or it's going to kill me.

Probably both.

Chapter 7
Rachel

I'm going to spontaneously combust from sexual frustration, and it's entirely Xander Ramsey's fault.

It's been a week since our encounter on the terrace—seven days of him stopping by the gallery with that predatory grace, sitting across from me during planning meetings while his ice-blue eyes undress me piece by torturous piece. Every "professional" interaction leaves me so wound up I could scream.

"Earth to Rachel," Peyton snaps her fingers in front of my face as we sit in our usual coffee shop booth. "You've been stirring that latte for five minutes. Either you're trying to achieve dairy enlightenment, or someone's got you twisted up like a pretzel."

"I'm fine," I lie, abandoning my over-stirred coffee. "Just stressed about the exhibition."

"Bullshit. You've got that glazed look people get when they're mentally undressing someone." Her eyes narrow with predatory interest. "Who is he? And more importantly, how big is his dick?"

"Peyton!"

"What? These are essential questions! You've been celibate so long I'm surprised cobwebs haven't formed. Clearly, someone's got your panties in a twist—literally, judging by how you keep squirming—so spill."

Heat creeps up my neck. "There's no one."

"Liar. You're practically vibrating with sexual energy." She leans forward conspiratorially. "Is it someone from the gallery? That cute guy with the man-bun who delivers art supplies? Or wait—" Her grin turns wicked. "Is it a collector? Some rich bastard who wants to add you to his private collection?"

My face flames so hot I probably look like a tomato having an allergic reaction.

"Holy fucking Christ, it IS a rich guy!" Peyton practically bounces in her seat. "Rachel Brooks, you absolute minx! Here I thought you were all innocent and pure, but you're lusting after some billionaire sugar daddy!"

"He's not a sugar daddy," I protest weakly.

"But he IS rich? And gorgeous? And making you forget how to form coherent sentences?" She studies my mortified expression. "Jesus, Rach, you've got it bad. When's the last time you actually got laid? Like, properly railed until you forgot your own name?"

"We are not discussing my sex life in public!"

"We absolutely are, because clearly your lady bits are staging a rebellion. You need to find this mystery millionaire and ride him until your vision goes blurry."

A woman at the next table chokes on her cappuccino. I want to dissolve into the floor.

"Look," Peyton continues, lowering her voice slightly, "you've been wound tighter than a drum since art school. When's the last time you let yourself actually want something? Someone?"

Before I can answer—or spontaneously die from embarrassment—my phone buzzes with a text from Julian: *Meeting with Xander at 3 PM to finalize exhibition layout. Don't be late.*

My stomach performs Olympic-level gymnastics.

An hour later, I'm sitting across from Xander in Julian's office, trying to focus on lighting diagrams while he explains optimal positioning for maximum visual impact. His voice is smooth and professional, but every time I glance up, his gaze is focused on my mouth like he's remembering exactly how I tasted.

"The center wall should feature your largest piece," he's saying, long fingers tracing the gallery layout. "It'll be the first thing visitors see when they enter."

"That's the one about yearning," I manage, my brain immediately conjuring the deep purples and midnight blues I painted after dreaming about his hands on my body.

"Perfect." His voice drops slightly. "Yearning deserves prominent placement."

The way he says 'yearning' makes my nipples tighten against my bra. I shift in my chair, trying to ignore the heat pooling between my thighs.

THE BILLIONAIRE'S MISTAKEN VOW

"And the lighting?" I ask, proud that my voice sounds relatively normal.

"Soft spotlights. Nothing harsh that might wash out the subtle color variations." He moves closer to point at the diagram, his shoulder brushing mine. "We want people to see every layer, every nuance you've created."

His cologne fills my nostrils—something expensive and masculine that makes my brain cells abandon ship. When he reaches across me to grab a pen, his forearm briefly presses against my breast.

The contact sends electricity shooting straight to my core.

"Sorry," he murmurs, but doesn't pull away immediately. His eyes meet mine, dark with unmistakable heat.

For a moment, we just stare at each other, the air crackling with tension. Then Julian's voice drifts through the glass partition, discussing framing options with Christina, and reality crashes back.

Xander straightens, his expression returning to professional neutrality. "We should also consider the promotional materials."

Right. Business. I can do business.

Except he keeps looking at me like he wants to spread me across this conference table and feast on me for hours.

After he leaves—with another lingering handshake that makes my knees wobble—Julian appears in the doorway wearing his concerned big-brother expression.

"We need to talk," he says, closing the door behind him.

My stomach sinks. "About what?"

"About whatever's happening between you and Xander." He settles into the chair Xander just vacated, his expression serious. "I care about you, Rachel. You're not just an employee—you're like family. And Xander... he's my brother, but he's also a predator when it comes to women."

"What? I mean—"

"Let me finish." He runs a hand through his hair. "Xander doesn't do relationships. He collects beautiful women like art pieces—displays them for a while, then moves on when he gets bored. Lauren Ashford lasted eighteen months, which is practically a marriage by his standards."

Each word feels like a punch to the gut. "I don't know what you think is happening—"

"I think my incredibly wealthy, devastatingly handsome older brother is showing unusual interest in a gorgeous, talented woman who works for me. And I think you're developing feelings that are going to get you hurt."

"We're just working together professionally," I lie.

"Bullshit. The sexual tension between you two could power half of Manhattan. I watched him nearly come unglued when Gael was flirting with you." Julian's expression softens. "Look, I'm not saying Xander's a bad guy. He's just... damaged. Our parents' divorces fucked him up pretty thoroughly. He doesn't trust easily, and he sure as hell doesn't let people get close."

"Thanks for the warning," I manage, my voice smaller than intended.

"I'm not trying to hurt you. I just don't want to watch Xander break your heart when he inevitably gets spooked and runs."

Three days later, I'm hiding in the gallery's storage room, surrounded by interview requests and media inquiries that make my anxiety spike to dangerous levels.

Art Monthly wants a feature story. Manhattan Modern requests a photo shoot. The Times is interested in your perspective on contemporary expressionism.

I stare at the growing pile of requests, my chest tightening with each one. These people want to interview me, photograph me, analyze my work in publications that sophisticated people read. What if I say something stupid? What if they realize I'm just a foster kid with more luck than talent?

"Shit, shit, shit," I mutter, pressing my palms against my eyes.

The storage room door opens, and I expect Christina or Julian, but Xander's concerned voice cuts through my panic.

"Rachel? What's wrong?"

I look up to find him crouched beside my makeshift fort of canvases and media requests, his perfect suit somehow unrumpled despite the cramped space.

"I can't do this," I whisper, gesturing at the interviews. "These people want to talk to a real artist, someone sophisticated and accomplished. Not some nobody who grew up bouncing between foster homes."

"Hey." His voice is gentle, understanding. "You're not a nobody."

"Yes, I am. I don't belong in their world, answering questions about artistic vision and contemporary relevance. They'll see right through me."

Without hesitation, Xander sinks to the floor beside me, his expensive suit be damned. "You want to know what I see when I look at your paintings?"

I shake my head, afraid to hear his answer.

"Honesty. Raw emotion that most people spend their entire lives trying to hide. Courage to put your vulnerability on display for the world to judge." His hand finds mine, warm and steady. "That's not nothing, Rachel. That's everything."

Tears prick my eyes. "But what if I'm not ready? What if I embarrass you, or the gallery, or—"

"You won't." His thumb traces gentle circles across my knuckles. "And even if you stumble, so what? You think every successful artist started out perfectly polished?"

"But you're investing so much money—"

"Because your work is worth it. Because you're worth it."

The sincerity in his voice breaks something open inside my chest. Before I can second-guess myself, I lean into him, needing his warmth and strength more than my next breath.

His arms come around me immediately, pulling me against his solid chest. I fit perfectly in the circle of his embrace, like I was designed specifically for this moment.

"Better?" he murmurs against my hair.

I nod, breathing in his expensive cologne mixed with something indefinably him. "Thank you."

"For what?"

"Making me feel like I matter."

His arms tighten around me. "You matter more than you know."

We sit like that in comfortable silence, surrounded by my art and the possibilities that terrify me. Gradually, I become aware of his heart beating steadily beneath my cheek, the way his breathing has synchronized with mine.

When I tilt my head to look at him, his face is closer than I expected. Close enough to count his dark eyelashes, to see the flecks of silver in his blue eyes.

Close enough to kiss.

His gaze drops to my mouth, and I watch his control slip another notch. One hand comes up to cup my face, thumb brushing across my lower lip.

My lips part involuntarily at the contact, and his pupils dilate.

He leans closer, and I rise to meet him halfway, every rational thought evaporating as the space between us disappears—

"Rachel, have you seen the—oh my God!"

We spring apart as Christina's shocked voice cuts through the tension like a machete. She stands in the storage room doorway, eyes wide with surprise and something that looks suspiciously like delight.

"I was just—we were discussing—" I stammer, my face burning with mortification.

"Exhibition details," Xander finishes smoothly, standing and offering me his hand. "Ms. Brooks was feeling overwhelmed by the media attention."

Christina's knowing smile could power a small city. "Of course. Very hands-on consultation, I see."

I want to crawl under the nearest canvas and die there.

"I should get back to work," I mumble, accepting Xander's help to stand on wobbling legs.

"Excellent idea," Christina says cheerfully. "Though you might want to fix your hair first. It looks a bit... tousled."

Holy fucking hell. If Christina noticed, how many other people have figured out that I'm completely gone for Xander Ramsey?

And more importantly, what the hell am I going to do about it?

Chapter 8
Xander

I can't concentrate for shit, and it's entirely Rachel Brooks' fault.

The way she melted against me in that storage room three days ago has completely fucked with my ability to focus on anything resembling actual work. During this morning's quarterly review, I spent forty-five minutes staring out the conference room window, mentally replaying how perfectly her soft curves fit against my chest.

"Xander, what's your take on the semiconductor projections?"

I blink, realizing twelve board members are waiting for my brilliant analysis while I've been daydreaming about auburn hair and vanilla perfume.

"Solid fundamentals," I manage, though I couldn't tell you what numbers we're discussing if my life depended on it. "Proceed with implementation."

Gael's knowing smirk could power half of Manhattan. The bastard can read me like a fucking roadmap.

"Riveting insight as always," he drawls once we're alone. "Very thorough. I especially enjoyed the drool pooling on your quarterly reports."

"I was thinking."

"With your cock, apparently." He drops into the chair beside me, thoroughly entertained. "So, when are you planning to nail the gallery girl? Because watching you eye-fuck empty air during budget meetings is getting pathetic."

"Her name is Rachel," I growl.

"Right, Rachel. The curvy redhead who's got Manhattan's most ruthless CEO twisted up like a fucking pretzel." His grin widens. "I'll bet you a thousand bucks you have her bent over that fancy desk of yours by Friday."

"You're disgusting."

"I'm realistic. You've been celibate for what, six months? And now there's this gorgeous artist making you forget how to form complete sentences." He leans back, studying my expression. "When's the last time you actually worked for a woman's attention instead of having them throw themselves at your bank account?"

Never. The answer is never, but I'm not giving him that ammunition.

"Two thousand says you chicken out," he continues. "All that Ice King reputation, but you're too scared to make a move on someone who might actually matter."

"Fuck off, Gael."

"Hit a nerve, did I?" He stands, straightening his expensive tie. "Look, I'm just saying—life's short, and she's gorgeous. Stop overthinking it and go get what you want."

THE BILLIONAIRE'S MISTAKEN VOW

What I want.

What I want is to taste every inch of Rachel's pale skin. What I want is to hear her moan my name while I make her forget every other man who's ever touched her. What I want is to wake up with her in my arms instead of alone in my cold penthouse.

But wanting something and having it are two very different things.

By seven PM, I'm prowling the gallery like a caged predator, telling myself I'm here to review exhibition logistics instead of hoping to catch a glimpse of Rachel working late on her pieces.

"You're becoming predictable," I mutter to myself, but push through the front door anyway.

The main lights are off, but soft illumination spills from the back workspace where she's probably lost in her art. I follow the glow like a moth to flame, my footsteps silent on the polished floors.

She's there, of course, completely absorbed in adding layers to a canvas that looks like liquid emotion. Her paint-splattered apron does nothing to hide her curves, and watching her move—unconsciously sensual as she reaches and bends and stretches—makes my blood run south.

"Working late again?" I ask softly.

She spins around, paintbrush flying from her startled fingers. "Jesus Christ! You scared the hell out of me!"

"Sorry." I'm not sorry at all. She looks fucking edible with her hair escaping its messy bun, a streak of cerulean blue across her left cheek. "Didn't mean to interrupt your process."

"It's fine. I was just adding some depth to the emotional landscape piece." She gestures at the canvas, suddenly shy. "Probably looks like a mess to someone used to sophisticated art."

"It looks like passion," I tell her honestly. "Like someone who understands that creating something beautiful requires bleeding parts of yourself onto the canvas."

Her eyes widen at my words. "That's... actually exactly what it feels like."

"Show me," I say, moving closer. "Explain how you translate feeling into color."

For the next twenty minutes, she guides me through her artistic process with growing confidence. Her insights about creative risk-taking mirror my own approach to business ventures—calculated chances that require trusting your instincts even when logic says otherwise.

"You know," she says, dabbing gold highlights onto the canvas, "the way you describe market analysis sounds similar to how I approach composition. Looking for patterns others miss, trusting your gut when the data doesn't tell the whole story."

"Exactly." I'm standing close enough to smell paint mixing with her vanilla perfume. "Most people think business is purely logical, but the best deals require intuition. Emotional intelligence."

"Like knowing when to push boundaries versus when to respect them?"

"Something like that." My voice drops as she turns to face me, those green eyes bright with understanding.

Thunder rumbles overhead, and suddenly the gallery plunges into complete darkness.

"Shit," she whispers. "Power must be out."

I use my phone's flashlight to locate the emergency candles Julian keeps in the supply closet, lighting several around her workspace. The flickering illumination transforms the gallery into something intimate and otherworldly.

"Better?" I ask.

"Much." But her voice sounds breathless as she watches me in the candlelight. "Though we probably shouldn't stay too late. Wouldn't want people to get the wrong idea."

"What kind of wrong idea?"

She blushes that gorgeous pink that makes me want to discover what other parts of her body turn that same shade. "You know exactly what kind."

"Maybe I want people to get the wrong idea."

The admission slips out before I can stop it, raw and honest in the flickering shadows.

"Xander..." she starts, but I'm already moving closer.

"I can't stop thinking about you," I confess, my voice rough with need. "The way you felt in my arms, how you taste, the little sounds you made when I touched you."

"We shouldn't—" But she doesn't pull away when I reach up to trace the paint streak on her cheek.

"Shouldn't what? Want each other? Because I'm pretty sure that ship has sailed."

She reaches for something on a high shelf, stretching up on her toes. The movement makes her lose balance, and I catch her automatically, pulling her against my chest.

This time, neither of us pulls away.

Her lips meet mine like coming home after years of wandering. She tastes like coffee and something indefinably sweet, and when she opens her mouth to let me deeper, I nearly lose my goddamn mind.

"Rachel," I breathe against her lips.

"Yes," she whispers back, understanding exactly what I'm asking.

I lift her onto the worktable, scattering paintbrushes and palette knives as I step between her legs. Her hands fist in my shirt, tugging at expensive buttons with desperate urgency.

"This is insane," she pants as I kiss down her throat.

"The best things usually are." I push her paint-stained apron aside, my hands exploring the soft curves I've been dreaming about. "God, you're so fucking beautiful."

Her response is lost as I capture her mouth again, pouring weeks of frustrated desire into the kiss. She arches against me, soft moans escaping her throat that drive me absolutely wild.

"I need to touch you," I growl, my hands sliding beneath her vintage dress.

"Please," she whimpers, and that single word destroys whatever restraint I had left.

I peel her dress over her head, revealing pale skin and curves that belong in a Renaissance painting. Her bra is simple white cotton, but the way her breasts threaten to spill over the cups makes my mouth water.

"Fucking perfect," I murmur, pressing hot kisses to the swells of her breasts.

"Xander, please, I need—" She tugs at my shirt until buttons scatter across the floor.

When her hands explore my chest, mapping muscle and scars with reverent touches, something primal takes over completely. I unhook her bra with practiced ease, then pause to worship what I've revealed.

"Your tits are incredible," I breathe, cupping the soft weight in my palms. "So responsive."

I lower my head to take one peaked nipple into my mouth, and she cries out sharply, her back arching off the table. The way she responds to my touch—completely uninhibited, purely instinctual—makes me harder than I've ever been.

"More," she gasps, her nails digging into my shoulders.

I lavish attention on her gorgeous breasts until she's writhing beneath me, desperate little sounds spilling from her lips. Then I trail kisses down her flat stomach, pausing at the waistband of her panties.

"These need to go," I tell her, hooking my fingers in the elastic.

She lifts her hips to help me slide them down her legs, and when I see her completely naked in the candlelight, surrounded by her art, I think I might actually die from want.

"You're the most beautiful thing I've ever seen," I tell her honestly.

"Stop talking and touch me," she demands, surprising us both with her boldness.

I spread her thighs wider, my thumbs stroking the sensitive skin until she's trembling with need. When I finally touch her where she's slick and ready, she nearly comes apart completely.

"So wet for me," I murmur, circling her clit with gentle pressure. "I've been dreaming about how you'd feel."

"Xander, I'm going to—oh God—"

I slide two fingers inside her while my thumb works her clit, and she shatters around me with a cry that echoes through the empty gallery. Watching her come undone is the most erotic thing I've ever witnessed.

Before she's fully recovered, I'm freeing myself from my pants, rolling on protection with shaking hands. When I position myself at her entrance, she opens those stunning green eyes and nods.

"I need you," she whispers.

I push inside slowly, both of us groaning at the exquisite sensation. She's tight and hot and perfect, and when she wraps her legs around my waist, I lose all semblance of control.

"Fuck, you feel incredible," I growl, starting to move.

"Harder," she gasps, meeting my thrusts with desperate urgency. "Please, Xander, I need—"

I give her what she needs, driving into her with increasing intensity until the worktable creaks beneath us. The sounds she makes—breathless moans and sharp cries of pleasure—push me closer to the edge with every stroke.

"That's it, baby," I encourage as she tightens around me. "Come for me again. Let me feel you."

When her second orgasm hits, the rhythmic pulses of her release trigger my own. I bury myself deep and come harder than I ever have, her name torn from my throat like a prayer.

We collapse together, breathing heavily as aftershocks continue to pulse through both our bodies. I gather her against my chest, pulling my suit jacket around her shoulders.

"That was..." she starts, then trails off.

"Yeah," I agree, understanding completely.

After a few minutes, she burrows deeper into my arms. "Xander? I need to tell you something."

"What is it, sweetheart?"

"I'm scared," she admits quietly. "I don't know how to be sophisticated enough for your world. All those collectors and critics at the exhibition—what if they see through me? What if I don't belong?"

Her vulnerability hits me square in the chest. Without thinking, I find myself sharing truths I've never spoken aloud.

"You want to know a secret?" I stroke her hair gently. "I'm lonely as hell most of the time. Success doesn't fill the empty spaces like people think it does. Most days, I go to bed in my penthouse overlooking the city, and all I can think about is how none of it means anything if you don't have someone to share it with."

She tilts her head to look at me, those green eyes soft with understanding. "Really?"

"Really. Money can buy almost anything, but it can't buy someone who sees past all the bullshit to who you actually are underneath." I cup her face gently. "You belong wherever you choose to be, Rachel. Anyone who can't see how extraordinary you are doesn't deserve your time."

She kisses me then, soft and sweet and full of promise. We arrange ourselves on the gallery couch, her body curved perfectly against mine as exhaustion finally claims us both.

I wake to early morning light streaming through the windows and Julian's shocked voice cutting through my peaceful haze.

"What the fuck is going on here?"

Shit.

Chapter 9
Rachel

Holy fucking Christ on a flaming cracker.

I scramble to pull Xander's suit jacket tighter around my naked body while Julian stands in the gallery doorway looking like he's witnessing the apocalypse in real time. His face cycles through approximately seventeen different emotions—shock, disgust, protective fury, and what looks suspiciously like homicidal rage.

"Julian," Xander says calmly, like being caught naked with his employee is just another Tuesday morning board meeting. "We can explain."

"Explain what exactly?" Julian's voice could freeze lava. "How you fucked my assistant on her workspace? How you manipulated a vulnerable woman for your sick entertainment?"

The words hit me like physical blows. Manipulated. Vulnerable. Entertainment.

"It's not like that," I whisper, but my voice comes out pathetically small.

"Isn't it?" Julian's gaze shifts to me, and the disappointment in his eyes makes my stomach curdle. "Jesus, Rachel. I warned you about him. I told you he collects women like art pieces."

"Julian, that's enough," Xander growls, standing and buttoning his shirt with infuriating composure.

"No, it's fucking not enough!" Julian explodes. "You saw an opportunity with someone who's never had money, never had anyone fight for her, and you pounced like the predator you are!"

Each accusation lands like a sledgehammer because they echo every insecurity I've spent my life trying to silence. Of course someone like Xander wouldn't genuinely want someone like me. Of course this was just another conquest.

"Stop," I manage, my throat tight with humiliation. "Please, just stop."

"And you," Julian continues, his fury now directed at me, "I can't believe you'd use your body to secure your exhibition placement. I thought you had more integrity than that."

The blood drains from my face completely. "That's not—I would never—"

"Wouldn't you? Convenient how Xander's sudden investment coincided with his obvious interest in getting into your pants."

I feel like I'm drowning in shame. The rational part of my brain knows Julian's lashing out from a place of protective concern, but his words are destroying what's left of my self-worth.

"Enough," Xander snarls, his voice deadly quiet. "You're way out of line."

"Am I? Because from where I'm standing, you just proved every terrible thing anyone's ever said about the Ramsey men."

THE BILLIONAIRE'S MISTAKEN VOW

Before Xander can respond—or potentially commit murder—Christina's voice cuts through the tension like a blade.

"What in the ever-loving hell is happening here?"

She appears in the doorway looking impeccable as always, but her expression shifts to protective mama-bear mode the second she takes in the scene: me clutching Xander's jacket, Julian radiating fury, Xander looking like he wants to demolish something with his bare hands.

"Julian was just explaining my moral failings," I say bitterly, finally finding my voice.

"Your moral failings?" Christina's perfectly sculpted eyebrows disappear into her hairline. "Julian Ramsey, you sanctimonious ass, what the fuck did you say to her?"

"I said what needed to be said. Xander manipulated her, and she—"

"She what? Made a choice about her own body and life? How fucking dare you shame her for being attracted to someone."

I want to disappear into the floor and never resurface. "Christina, please—"

"No, honey. This is bullshit." She turns her laser focus on Julian. "Rachel's a grown woman who can sleep with whoever she damn well pleases without your moral commentary."

"Even if it compromises her professional integrity?" Julian shoots back.

"Especially then," Christina snaps. "Because newsflash: men have been mixing business and pleasure since the dawn of fucking time without anyone questioning their professional integrity."

I can't take it anymore. The accusations, the defending, the way they're all talking about me like I'm not standing right here—it's too much.

"Stop," I say firmly, surprising everyone including myself. "All of you, just stop."

I gather my clothes from where they're scattered across the floor, dignity be damned. "I need to get dressed and get out of here."

"Rachel—" Xander starts, but I cut him off.

"Don't. Just... don't."

I escape to the bathroom, pulling on my wrinkled dress with shaking hands. In the mirror, I look thoroughly fucked—hair a disaster, lips swollen, paint still streaking my cheek. The evidence of my poor life choices written across my face for everyone to see.

When I emerge, Julian and Xander are engaged in a heated whispered argument while Christina examines her perfectly manicured nails with studied nonchalance.

"I'm leaving," I announce.

"We need to talk about this," Xander says, moving toward me.

"No, we really don't." I grab my purse and jacket, desperate to escape before I completely fall apart in front of everyone.

THE BILLIONAIRE'S MISTAKEN VOW

Christina follows me outside, her heels clicking authoritatively on the sidewalk.

"Rachel, wait."

I stop, mainly because my legs are shaking too badly to continue walking.

"Look," she says gently, "Julian's a protective idiot, but he's not entirely wrong about one thing."

My heart sinks. "Which thing?"

"Dating Xander Ramsey comes with brutal reality checks. The media attention, the social pressure, the constant speculation about your motives—it's fucking relentless."

"So, you think I should—"

"I think you should be prepared. You're about to become tabloid fodder. 'Billionaire's New Plaything,' 'Gold Digger Bags Another Rich Boy'—that kind of charming bullshit."

The thought makes my stomach churn. "Maybe Julian's right. Maybe I should end this before it gets worse."

"Or maybe you should decide what you actually want instead of letting fear make your choices." Christina's expression softens. "I've seen you with him. That wasn't manipulation—that was two people who are completely gone for each other."

"But what if—"

"What if he breaks your heart? What if the media destroys your reputation? What if you're not sophisticated enough for his world?" She counts off my fears on perfectly manicured fingers. "Honey, all of those things might happen. The question is: is he worth the risk?"

An hour later, I'm sprawled on Peyton's couch with a bottle of tequila and a rapidly deteriorating sense of dignity.

"That pretentious douchebag!" Peyton rages, pacing her tiny living room like a caged tiger. "How dare Julian slut-shame you for getting your pussy worshipped by a gorgeous billionaire!"

"He wasn't slut-shaming—"

"The fuck he wasn't! 'Using your body to secure your exhibition'—that's grade-A slut-shaming wrapped in concern-trolling bullshit."

I take another swig of tequila, hoping alcohol will numb the humiliation. "Maybe he has a point though. The timing looks suspicious."

"Rachel Brooks, if you internalize that misogynistic garbage, I'm staging an intervention." Peyton stops pacing to fix me with her most serious expression. "Tell me exactly what happened last night. Every detail."

So I do. I tell her about the candlelight, the way Xander looked at my paintings like they mattered, how gentle he was when I confessed my fears. I describe the way he touched me—reverent, desperate, like I was precious—and how he shared his own vulnerability afterward.

"Jesus fucking Christ," Peyton breathes when I finish. "That wasn't casual sex. That was making love."

THE BILLIONAIRE'S MISTAKEN VOW

"It was just—"

"It was not 'just' anything. That man is completely head-over-heels for you." She drops onto the couch beside me. "The question is: what are you going to do about it?"

"Run away to a different country and change my name?"

"Wrong answer. You're going to march your ass back there and fight for what you want." Peyton grabs my shoulders. "When has running away ever gotten you anything except more loneliness?"

Before I can argue, my phone buzzes with a delivery notification. Twenty minutes later, I'm staring at the most gorgeous floral arrangement I've ever seen—exotic orchids and roses that probably cost more than my rent.

The card reads: *Please let me explain. You matter more than you know. - X*

"Holy shit," Peyton whistles. "Those are some serious 'please forgive me' flowers."

"Or 'thanks for the fuck' flowers," I mutter, but my heart is doing stupid fluttery things.

"Don't be dense. Men don't send flowers like these for casual hookups." She examines the arrangement like she's appraising diamonds. "These are 'I'm falling in love with you' flowers."

I spend the rest of the day drowning myself in exhibition preparations, arranging and rearranging my pieces until my hands are cramped and my brain is numb. If I stay busy enough, maybe I won't think about how perfect it felt to fall asleep in Xander's arms.

Julian shows up at the gallery around five with coffee and a sheepish expression.

"We need to discuss damage control," he says carefully.

"Meaning?"

"Meaning maybe you should step back from working directly with Xander. I can handle all the remaining exhibition coordination."

The suggestion hits me like a slap. "You want to sideline me from my own showcase?"

"I want to protect you from getting hurt worse than you already have been."

"I'm not a child, Julian. I can make my own decisions about my relationships and my career."

"Can you? Because this morning suggested otherwise."

The condescension in his tone makes my temper flare. "You know what? Fuck your protection. I don't need you managing my life like I'm some helpless foster kid who can't navigate the big scary world."

Julian flinches. "That's not what I meant—"

"It's exactly what you meant. You see me as someone who needs saving from her own poor judgment." I gather my things with sharp, angry movements. "Well, newsflash: I survived eighteen years in the system without your help. I think I can handle one complicated billionaire."

"Rachel, please—"

But I'm already walking out of the gallery, my second dramatic exit of the day.

The next morning brings a special kind of hell: my phone won't stop buzzing with notifications. *Manhattan Socialite*, *Elite Weekly*, and half a dozen gossip blogs are all running speculation pieces about "Xander Ramsey's Latest Conquest."

Who is the mysterious redhead spotted at the billionaire's gallery rendezvous?

Gallery Girl: Another Notch in Ramsey's Belt?

From Foster Care to Fifth Avenue: The Cinderella Story That Has Manhattan Talking

Each headline makes me want to vomit. They've dug up my background, my financial struggles, even found photos from my art school graduation. The comments sections are brutal—calling me a gold digger, a social climber, worse things I don't want to repeat.

"This is exactly what I was afraid of," I whisper to my empty apartment.

My phone rings. Christina's name flashes on the screen.

"Have you seen the gossip sites?" she asks without preamble.

"Unfortunately."

"It's going to get worse before it gets better. Xander Ramsey's dating life is considered prime entertainment for Manhattan's elite." Her voice gentles. "How are you holding up?"

"I feel like I'm drowning in other people's opinions about my life."

"Welcome to dating a billionaire. It's like being a reality TV star except you never auditioned for the show."

A knock at my door interrupts our conversation. I peek through the peephole and nearly drop my phone.

Xander stands in my dingy hallway looking like a GQ cover model who wandered into the wrong neighborhood. His expensive suit makes my building's chipped paint and flickering fluorescent lights look even more pathetic by comparison.

"He's here," I whisper to Christina.

"Who's where?"

"Xander. At my door. Looking like he stepped out of a fucking magazine shoot."

"Answer it, you coward."

"I can't. I look like I haven't slept in days and I'm wearing my rattiest pajamas."

"Answer the fucking door, Rachel."

Another knock, more insistent this time.

"Rachel," Xander's voice carries through the thin door. "I know you're in there. Please, let me explain before you make any decisions you'll regret."

My heart hammers against my ribs. He's seen the gossip articles. He knows I know that our private moment has become public entertainment.

And he's here anyway.

"I have to go," I tell Christina.

"Fight for what you want," she says firmly before hanging up.

I take a deep breath, smooth down my hair, and open the door to face whatever comes next.

Chapter 10
Xander

Standing in this dingy hallway clutching takeout from Rachel's favorite Thai place—information I bribed out of Peyton with promises of expensive wine and entirely too many crude jokes about my sexual performance—I feel like I'm about to pitch the most important deal of my life.

Except this isn't about profit margins or market dominance. This is about convincing the woman who's completely scrambled my brain that I'm not the heartless bastard my reputation suggests.

When she opens the door, my chest tightens painfully. She looks exhausted, her auburn hair escaping a messy ponytail, wearing oversized pajamas that somehow make her even more beautiful than the elegant dress she wore to the gala.

"You brought food," she says quietly, like she's surprised someone would think of her basic needs.

"Pad Thai with extra peanuts, spring rolls, and that mango sticky rice you apparently devour when stressed." I hold up the bags. "Peyton's very descriptive when properly motivated."

"You bribed my best friend?"

"Extensively. She also shared several graphic theories about our sexual compatibility that I'm choosing to interpret as encouragement rather than threats."

The ghost of a smile tugs at her lips. "That sounds like Peyton."

She steps aside to let me in, and Christ, her apartment tells me more about who she really is than months of professional interaction ever could. Canvases line every available wall, brushes scattered across makeshift tables, a vintage velvet couch that's seen better decades but somehow looks perfectly her.

It's cramped and chaotic and absolutely nothing like the sterile perfection of my penthouse, and I've never wanted to belong somewhere more desperately in my entire life.

"It's not much," she says, suddenly self-conscious as she watches me take in her space.

"It's perfect," I tell her honestly. "It's completely, authentically you."

We settle on her couch with the food spread between us like a peace offering. For several minutes, we eat in comfortable silence while I figure out how to explain that everything Julian accused me of is simultaneously true and completely wrong.

"About yesterday morning," I start.

"Don't." She sets down her chopsticks, green eyes guarded. "I've had time to think, and Julian wasn't entirely off base. The timing of your investment, then us sleeping together—it looks calculated as hell."

"It wasn't calculated. It was the opposite of calculated." I run a hand through my hair, struggling to find words that don't sound like corporate bullshit. "You want honesty? I've been completely out of control since the moment you ran from my penthouse in that wet dress."

"Out of control how? Because from where I'm sitting, everything seems to benefit you pretty fucking conveniently."

Her crude language shouldn't turn me on, but it absolutely does. "You think sleeping with you benefits me? You think I'm enjoying having my every move scrutinized by gossip rags and my own brother questioning my motives?"

"Aren't you? Another conquest, another beautiful woman who'll disappear when you get bored?"

The pain in her voice hits me like a physical blow. "Is that really what you think? That you're just another fucking conquest?"

"What else am I supposed to think? Look at this place." She gestures around her tiny apartment. "Look at me. I clip coupons and wear thrift store dresses and eat ramen for dinner. You collect art worth more than my yearly income."

"And that matters why exactly?"

"Because people like you don't fall for people like me. You might enjoy slumming it temporarily, but eventually you'll remember where you belong."

Her words expose wounds so deep I can practically see them bleeding. Every foster home that didn't want her permanently, every temporary placement that reinforced her belief that she's not worth keeping.

THE BILLIONAIRE'S MISTAKEN VOW

"You want to know what scares the shit out of me?" I lean forward, needing her to understand. "It's not your background or your bank account or your fucking thrift store wardrobe. It's how much I need you."

"Need me for what? Amazing sex? Someone different to spice up your boring billionaire existence?"

"Need you to breathe," I say roughly. "Need you to remember why money and success matter if there's no one to share them with. Need you to look at me like I'm just Xander instead of some corporate machine."

Her breath catches slightly, but she doesn't back down. "Pretty words. Your reputation suggests they come easy to you."

Before I can respond, my phone starts buzzing insistently. Gael's name flashes on the screen, and I consider letting it go to voicemail until Rachel nods toward it.

"Answer it. I'll wait."

I swipe to accept, putting it on speaker before Gael can launch into something truly offensive.

"Xander, you magnificent bastard," his voice fills the small space, "please tell me you're not actually dating that gallery girl. The betting pool at the club has reached obscene levels."

Rachel's face goes white. I want to murder my best friend with my bare hands.

"Gael—"

"Because seriously, slumming with struggling artists is one thing, but the media's making this look like an actual relationship. You're not going soft on me, are you?"

"Shut the fuck up," I snarl, my voice deadly quiet. "Right fucking now."

The silence stretches for exactly three seconds before he speaks again, his tone completely different. "Holy shit. You're serious about her."

"Dead serious. And if I hear you or anyone else refer to Rachel as 'slumming' again, I'll destroy you professionally and personally. Are we crystal fucking clear?"

"Crystal. Jesus, Xander, I didn't realize—"

"You didn't realize because you never bothered asking. Rachel isn't some temporary diversion. She's the most important thing in my life, and anyone who can't respect that can find new friends."

I hang up without waiting for his response, my chest heaving with protective fury.

Rachel stares at me with wide eyes. "You just threatened your best friend. For me."

"I'd threaten the entire fucking city for you." The admission slips out raw and honest. "You want proof this isn't some calculated seduction? There it is. I just burned bridges with half my social circle to defend your honor."

"Xander..." she whispers.

"I'm not perfect, Rachel. I've made mistakes, hurt people, chosen work over relationships more times than I can count. But what happened between us—that was real. The way you feel in my arms, the way you challenge me, the way you make me want to be better—none of that's an act."

She sets down her food completely, studying my face like she's searching for lies. "What happens when the novelty wears off? When you remember I don't know which fork to use at fancy dinners?"

"Then I'll teach you about forks. Or better yet, we'll eat with our hands and scandalize everyone." I reach for her hands, relieved when she doesn't pull away. "I don't want someone who already fits my world perfectly. I want someone who makes me question why that world matters."

"The media attention will get worse," she says quietly.

"Probably. Which is why I'm having my PR team draft statements to control the narrative. Professional photos, carefully worded releases, whatever it takes to protect your reputation."

Her eyes widen. "You'd do that?"

"I'm already doing it. Called them before I came over." I brush my thumb across her knuckles. "Your career matters to me because you matter to me. I won't let gossip columnists destroy what you've worked so hard to build."

For long moments, we sit in silence while she processes everything. Finally, she speaks.

"I'm terrified you'll leave when things get complicated. Everyone always leaves when I become inconvenient."

"I'm terrified you'll run before giving us a real chance," I admit. "That you'll let fear make decisions for you instead of trusting what's happening between us."

"So what do we do?"

"We take it slow. We're careful about public appearances until the media frenzy dies down. We communicate instead of assuming the worst about each other's motives." I lift her hand to my lips, pressing a gentle kiss to her palm. "And we stop letting other people's opinions dictate our choices."

She nods slowly. "I can try that."

"That's all I'm asking."

When I kiss her goodnight at her door—soft and tender and full of promises neither of us is ready to voice—she melts against me like she belongs there.

"Tomorrow's going to bring new challenges," I murmur against her forehead.

"Probably. But maybe we'll figure it out together."

I'm halfway home when hope blooms in my chest for the first time in years. Rachel Brooks might just be brave enough to take a chance on us.

The next morning, my phone's buzzing insistently drags me from the deepest sleep I've had in months. Julian's name flashes repeatedly across the screen, and the early hour suggests crisis-level urgency.

"What's wrong?" I answer without preamble.

"We've got a problem," Julian's voice is tight with stress. "Lauren's back in town, and she's been asking very pointed questions about your new relationship. Apparently, she's 'concerned about your reputation' and wants to meet the artist who's 'taking advantage' of your generous nature."

Ice floods my veins. Lauren Ashford—manipulative, calculating, and completely ruthless when she doesn't get what she wants.

"Fuck," I breathe, already reaching for clothes.

"Yeah. And Xander? She specifically asked for Rachel's home address."

Chapter 11
Rachel

"Holy fucking Christ, you look like a sex goddess who moonlights as an artist," Peyton declares, stepping back to admire her styling handiwork. "That dress is basically foreplay in fabric form."

I stare at myself in the mirror, barely recognizing the woman looking back. The midnight blue silk clings to every curve Xander's hands have memorized, and the plunging neckline suggests rather than reveals. It's sophisticated enough for Manhattan's art elite but sexy enough to make my billionaire boyfriend forget his own name.

"You think it's too much?" I ask, adjusting the neckline for the hundredth time.

"Honey, after the way that man rearranged your internal organs last week, nothing is too much." Peyton grins wickedly. "Besides, great dick has given you this confidence that's absolutely radiating from your pores. Your art's gotten bolder, your posture's straighter, and you've stopped apologizing for taking up space."

Heat creeps up my neck. "Can we not discuss my sex life while I'm having a nervous breakdown?"

"We absolutely can, because orgasms are clearly your secret artistic weapon. That painting you finished yesterday? Pure post-coital genius. I'm pretty sure you captured the essence of getting thoroughly fucked in abstract form."

"Peyton!"

"What? I'm being supportive! Xander Ramsey's magical penis has unlocked your creative potential. It's beautiful, really."

Before I can murder my best friend, my phone buzzes with a text from Xander: *You're going to be incredible tonight. I can't wait to watch everyone fall in love with your art the way I've fallen for the artist.*

My stomach performs gymnastic routines that would impress Olympic judges.

"Aww, he's being adorable again," Peyton reads over my shoulder. "I still can't believe you bagged a billionaire who sends romantic texts instead of dick pics."

An hour later, I'm standing in the gallery watching Christina direct the final touches on my exhibition setup. My paintings glow under perfectly positioned spotlights, each piece positioned to create maximum emotional impact. The yearning landscape—deep purples and midnight blues born from dreams about ice-blue eyes—commands the center wall like a declaration of desire.

"This is it," I whisper to myself. "This is actually happening."

"Talking to yourself is the first sign of artistic genius," a smooth female voice says behind me. "Or complete mental breakdown. Either way, very authentic."

I turn to find a woman who looks like she stepped off the cover of Vogue. Platinum blonde hair falls in perfect waves past her shoulders, her angular face showcasing cheekbones that could cut glass. Her designer dress probably cost more than my yearly rent, and she moves with the predatory grace of someone accustomed to getting exactly what she wants.

"I don't think we've been introduced," she continues, extending a manicured hand. "Lauren Ashford. I'm sure Xander's mentioned me."

My blood turns to ice water. This is Lauren. Xander's ex. The sophisticated socialite who lasted eighteen months in his life—practically a marriage by his standards, according to Julian.

"Rachel Brooks," I manage, shaking her perfectly soft hand.

"Of course. The artist." Her smile is sharp enough to perform surgery. "Your work is so... emotional. Very raw. I imagine it takes tremendous courage to expose yourself so completely to public scrutiny."

The way she says 'expose yourself' makes it sound vaguely pornographic.

"Art requires vulnerability," I reply carefully.

"Indeed. Though I have to admire your boldness, diving into Xander's world so quickly. Most people find the transition from... modest circumstances... to his social circle rather overwhelming."

Each word is perfectly polite and absolutely venomous. She's dissecting my background, making it clear she knows exactly where I come from and how little I belong here.

"Rachel's handling everything beautifully," Christina interjects, appearing at my elbow like a glamorous guardian angel. "Lauren, what a surprise. I thought you were in the Hamptons."

"Just returned this morning. When I heard about Xander's latest... investment... I simply had to see for myself what's captured his attention so thoroughly."

The pause before 'investment' makes my skin crawl.

"Well, you'll have plenty of opportunity to admire her work tonight," Christina says smoothly. "The collector turnout is expected to be exceptional."

"I'm sure it will be. Xander always draws quite the crowd when he publicly supports emerging talent." Lauren's gaze travels over my dress with obvious assessment. "That's a lovely choice, by the way. Very... accessible."

Accessible. Like I'm a fucking community college instead of a woman.

After Lauren glides away to terrorize other victims, Christina grabs my arm with barely contained fury.

"That venomous bitch," she hisses. "I should have warned you she was in town."

"You know her?"

"Know her? Honey, I've watched Lauren Ashford destroy three of Xander's previous relationships through strategic social warfare. She's like a beautiful, well-dressed plague."

My stomach drops. "What do you mean, destroy?"

"Subtle sabotage disguised as concern. She plants seeds of doubt about compatibility, stages 'accidental' encounters that highlight class differences, makes the other woman feel so inadequate they usually end things themselves."

"And it works?"

"Like a fucking charm. The woman has a PhD in psychological manipulation." Christina's expression turns fierce. "But those other women weren't you. They didn't have your backbone or your talent or your ability to make Xander look at them like they hung the goddamn moon."

Before I can process that completely, Julian calls for final sound checks. The next two hours blur together in a whirlwind of arriving guests, clinking champagne glasses, and art collectors examining my soul painted on canvas.

Then Xander arrives, and the entire room shifts.

He commands attention without trying—that lethal combination of power and sex appeal that makes conversations pause mid-sentence. His charcoal suit fits his tall frame like liquid sin, and when his ice-blue eyes find mine across the crowded gallery, everything else fades to background noise.

He moves through the crowd with practiced ease, shaking hands and making small talk while steadily working his way toward me. Every step broadcasts ownership and pride in a way that makes my pulse race and my panties dampen.

"There's my brilliant artist," he murmurs when he finally reaches me, pressing a soft kiss to my temple that feels like claiming.

"You're late," I tease, though his presence immediately calms my jangled nerves.

"Traffic. Besides, I wanted to make an entrance worthy of the woman I'm here to celebrate."

His arm slides around my waist, pulling me against his side where I fit perfectly. The gesture is possessive and protective, broadcasting to everyone present that I'm his and he's damn proud of it.

"Xander!" Lauren's voice cuts through our moment like a blade. "Darling, you look magnificent. Success always suited you beautifully."

She kisses both his cheeks in a gesture that's European and intimate, her hands lingering on his lapels longer than strictly necessary. Standing next to her, I feel like a bargain basement knockoff beside the original designer piece.

"Lauren." His voice is polite but distant. "I wasn't expecting to see you here."

"How could I miss supporting emerging talent? Besides, we have so much catching up to do. It's been months since we've had a proper conversation."

The way she says 'proper conversation' suggests they used to have many improper ones.

"I'm exactly where I need to be," Xander replies, his arm tightening around me.

"Of course. Though I'd love to steal you away for just a moment to discuss the Henderson Foundation gala. They're still hoping you'll co-chair the committee."

She's doing it. Right in front of me, she's using their shared social connections to claim his attention and remind everyone that she belongs in his world in ways I never will.

"Perhaps later," he says, but she's already linking her arm through his free one.

"It'll just take a moment. Rachel won't mind, will you, darling? Artists understand the importance of networking."

Before I can object, she's steering him toward a group of older collectors, leaving me standing alone while they discuss charity events and social obligations I've never heard of.

Watching them together is like witnessing a perfectly choreographed dance. Lauren knows exactly which stories to reference, which mutual friends to mention, how to make Xander laugh with inside jokes I'll never understand. They look natural together in a way that makes my chest ache with inadequacy.

"Don't let her get in your head," Christina whispers, appearing beside me with fresh champagne. "That's exactly what she wants."

"Look at them," I whisper back. "They fit together like puzzle pieces. She knows his world, his friends, his history."

"And you know his heart. Which piece matters more?"

Before I can answer, a distinguished gentleman approaches my yearning landscape painting, studying it with obvious fascination.

"Extraordinary work," he tells me when I join him. "There's such hunger in the brushstrokes. Such longing. It reminds me of Rothko's later pieces, but with more sensuality."

"Thank you," I manage, trying to focus on the compliment instead of watching Lauren monopolize Xander's attention.

"I'd like to make an offer. Would fifty thousand be acceptable?"

My champagne glass slips from suddenly nerveless fingers. Fifty thousand dollars. For one painting. More money than I've ever seen in my life.

"I... yes. Absolutely yes."

The next hour passes in a blur of red dots appearing next to my pieces, collectors discussing commissions, and critics asking about my artistic influences. Seven paintings sell, including the yearning landscape that started this whole journey.

When Xander finally extricates himself from Lauren's clutches, his expression is thunderous.

"I'm sorry," he says immediately. "She cornered me, and I couldn't be rude without causing a scene."

"It's fine," I lie, watching Lauren hold court near the champagne fountain. "She's beautiful. And she obviously cares about you."

"She cares about the lifestyle I provide. There's a difference." His hands frame my face, forcing me to meet his gaze. "You sold seven pieces tonight. Seven. You're officially a successful artist, and I've never been prouder of anyone in my entire life."

His obvious pride melts some of my insecurity, but Lauren's presence continues hovering at the edges of my consciousness like a perfectly dressed storm cloud.

The evening winds down with promises of future exhibitions and magazine interviews. As guests begin filtering out, I allow myself to feel genuinely proud of what I've accomplished.

Then Lauren appears at my elbow while Xander's occupied with Julian, her smile sharp as surgical steel.

"Congratulations on your little triumph," she says sweetly. "Though I suppose I should offer some friendly advice, woman to woman."

"What kind of advice?"

"About Xander. You see, I've known him for years, watched his patterns with artistic types like yourself. The intense fascination, the generous investments, the way he makes you feel like you're the center of his universe." Her laugh is silver and deadly. "It's quite intoxicating while it lasts."

"What are you trying to say?"

"I'm saying enjoy it while you can, darling. Because Xander always comes back to what's familiar. What fits. What makes sense in his world." She steps closer, her voice dropping to a whisper. "He's had three artist girlfriends before you. Painters, sculptors, even a performance artist. Each one thought she was different, special, the one who would finally hold his attention permanently."

My blood turns to ice. "And?"

"And they're all footnotes now. Distant memories he recalls fondly while he's back with someone suitable. Someone like me." Her smile could freeze lava. "So by all means, enjoy your moment in the spotlight. Just don't mistake temporary fascination for lasting love."

Chapter 12
Xander

I watch Lauren work the room like a goddamn predator in designer heels, and every manipulative move she makes sends ice through my veins. She's using the same playbook that nearly destroyed my confidence years ago—the subtle digs disguised as concern, the possessive touches disguised as friendly affection, the way she positions herself like she belongs at my side.

Not happening. Not this time. Not with Rachel.

"Mr. Ramsey," Damon Wellington, one of Manhattan's most influential collectors, approaches with obvious curiosity. "I'm absolutely fascinated by Ms. Brooks' work. Such raw emotion. How did you discover her?"

Before I can answer, Lauren materializes beside us like a fucking social parasite. "Oh, Damon, darling! Xander's always had such an eye for emerging talent. Remember that sculptor from Tribeca he was so passionate about? What was her name again?"

"Ms. Brooks is extraordinary," I say firmly, my voice carrying enough ice to freeze Lauren's manipulative smile. "Her talent speaks for itself, which is why seven collectors have already made purchases tonight.

Her success has nothing to do with our personal relationship and everything to do with her exceptional artistic vision."

Damon nods appreciatively. "Indeed. That yearning landscape piece—I've never seen such sophisticated use of color to convey emotional depth."

"Rachel creates from authentic experience," I continue, making sure Lauren hears every word. "There's no pretense in her work, no calculated appeal to trends. Just honest vulnerability that most artists spend their entire careers trying to achieve."

Lauren's smile turns razor-sharp. "How wonderfully supportive you are, Xander. Though I do hope the poor dear isn't overwhelmed by all this attention. Sometimes sudden success can be quite destabilizing for artists from more... humble backgrounds."

That's it. I'm done with her passive-aggressive bullshit.

"Excuse us, Damon," I say politely, then grip Lauren's elbow and steer her toward the gallery's back corridor with barely controlled fury.

"What the fuck are you doing here?" I demand once we're out of earshot.

"Supporting emerging artists, of course." Her innocent act would be impressive if I hadn't endured eighteen months of her manipulation. "Though I am concerned about you, darling. This pattern of yours with creative types—"

"There's no pattern."

"Really? The painter from Chelsea, the ceramicist from Brooklyn, that performance artist who did those dreadful installations?" She counts them off on perfectly manicured fingers. "Each one thought she was special, the one who would finally tame the great Xander Ramsey."

"And yet I'm here with Rachel, not reminiscing about past mistakes."

Her mask slips slightly, revealing the calculating bitch underneath. "Past mistakes? Is that what you call our eighteen months together?"

"I call it a learning experience. One that taught me the difference between genuine connection and sophisticated manipulation."

"How cruel you've become." She steps closer, her perfume cloying and familiar. "We were perfect together, Xander. Same background, same social circle, same understanding of what matters in this world."

"We were toxic together. You spent eighteen months trying to mold me into your ideal accessory while I convinced myself that compatibility meant settling for someone who treated love like a business transaction."

"And this little artist is different? She won't want your money, your connections, your lifestyle?" Lauren's laugh is silver and vicious. "Darling, they always want those things eventually."

"Rachel's not them. And I'm sure as hell not the man who was stupid enough to think you were worth eighteen months of my life."

I walk away before she can respond, but the damage is already done. Across the gallery, I watch Rachel's shoulders tense as she processes whatever poison Lauren whispered in her ear during my absence.

Fuck. I know that look—the way her walls are rebuilding themselves brick by brick, how she's already preparing to run before I can disappoint her.

The rest of the evening passes in a blur of congratulations and business cards, but all I can focus on is the growing distance in Rachel's green eyes. She smiles and thanks collectors for their purchases, but there's a fragility to her composure that makes me want to hunt Lauren down and explain exactly why threatening my woman is a career-limiting move.

By the time the last guest filters out, Rachel looks exhausted and hollow despite her professional triumph.

"Come home with me," I say quietly, helping her gather her things.

"Xander, I should probably—"

"Come home with me," I repeat, more firmly this time. "We need to talk, and you need to decompress somewhere that isn't filled with memories of whatever toxic shit Lauren fed you tonight."

She hesitates, and I watch doubt war with desire across her beautiful face.

"Please," I add, because pride means nothing when she's looking at me like I might disappear at any moment.

Thirty minutes later, we're in my penthouse with the city glittering beneath us like fallen stars. I've poured expensive wine and lit candles, creating an intimate atmosphere that should celebrate her incredible success.

Instead, she stands by the windows looking lost and smaller than I've ever seen her.

"Seven paintings sold," I say, coming up behind her. "That's fucking extraordinary for a debut exhibition."

"Is it? Or is it just what happens when you sleep with the right investor?"

The pain in her voice hits me like a sledgehammer to the chest. "You think your talent is somehow less valid because we're together?"

"I think Lauren made some very compelling points about your history with artistic types."

I turn her to face me, my hands gentle on her shoulders. "What exactly did she say?"

"That you have a pattern. That you've done this before with other artists, made them feel special and important until the novelty wore off."

"And you believed her."

"Why shouldn't I? Look at us, Xander. Look at this place." She gestures around my penthouse with its museum-quality art and million-dollar views. "You live in a different stratosphere. What happens when you remember that I'm nobody special?"

"You want to know about my history with artists?" I guide her to the couch, pouring more wine while I choose my words carefully. "Yes, I've dated creative women before. Three of them, to be precise. Want to know why those relationships ended?"

She nods, steeling herself for confirmation of her worst fears.

"Because they wanted what Lauren accused them of wanting. The lifestyle, the connections, the financial security. Each one gradually stopped creating their own art and started curating themselves to fit my world instead."

"And that's different from what I'm doing how?"

"Because you're still fighting me every step of the way. Because you'd rather eat ramen than accept help with your rent. Because you ran from my penthouse in a panic instead of trying to seduce me for my money." I cup her face, forcing her to meet my gaze. "Because you sold seven paintings tonight based on pure talent, and you're still worried you don't deserve success."

"Lauren said—"

"Lauren's a manipulative bitch who spent eighteen months trying to convince me that love meant changing everything about myself to fit her image of the perfect boyfriend." My voice hardens with remembered resentment. "She's terrified that someone authentic might succeed where her calculated perfection failed."

"But she knows your world—"

"She knows how to navigate social bullshit and charity galas. You know how to create something beautiful from nothing but raw emotion and pigment." I lean closer, my lips brushing her temple. "Which skill do you think matters more to someone who's spent his entire life surrounded by beautiful, empty things?"

For long moments, we sit in silence while she processes my words. Finally, she speaks.

"I'm scared, Xander. Not just of Lauren or the media attention. I'm scared of needing you too much, of becoming someone who can't function without your support."

"Good. Because I'm scared of the same thing—needing you so much that I'd compromise everything to keep you." I stroke her hair gently. "Maybe being scared means we're taking this seriously enough."

She tilts her head to look at me, those green eyes bright with unshed tears. "What if we're too different? What if this ends badly and ruins everything?"

"Then we'll deal with it together. But Rachel—" I lean down to kiss her softly. "I'd rather risk everything with you than play it safe with someone who doesn't make me feel alive."

Her lips part under mine, and suddenly we're kissing with desperate hunger, months of emotional buildup exploding into pure need. She tastes like wine and possibility, and when she moans against my mouth, every rational thought evacuates my brain.

"I need you," she whispers, her hands fumbling with my shirt buttons.

"Thank fuck," I breathe, lifting her against me. "Because I've been dying to worship your gorgeous body properly."

I carry her to my bedroom, laying her gently on silk sheets while I take my time removing her dress. The candlelight from the living room casts dancing shadows across her pale skin, and she looks like a masterpiece come to life.

"You're so fucking beautiful," I murmur, pressing kisses to her throat. "Every inch of you drives me crazy."

My hands explore her curves with reverent touches, reacquainting themselves with every sensitive spot that makes her arch and gasp. When I take her nipple into my mouth, she cries out sharply, her nails digging into my shoulders.

"Xander, please—"

"Please what, sweetheart?" I switch to her other breast, lavishing equal attention until she's writhing beneath me.

"Touch me. Everywhere. I need to feel how much you want me."

I spend the next twenty minutes doing exactly that, using hands and mouth to bring her to the edge repeatedly before backing off. By the time I finally slide two fingers inside her slick heat, she's practically sobbing with need.

"That's it, baby," I encourage, watching her face as I work her closer to climax. "Let me see how beautiful you look when you fall apart for me."

Her orgasm hits like a tidal wave, her entire body convulsing as she screams my name. The sight of her coming undone in my bed is the most erotic thing I've ever witnessed.

Before she's fully recovered, I'm positioning myself between her thighs, but she stops me with gentle hands.

"My turn," she insists, pushing me onto my back.

"Rachel—"

"Let me show you how much you mean to me."

She takes me into her mouth with obvious enthusiasm, and Christ, the way she looks up at me while she works her magic nearly stops my heart. But I need to be inside her more than I need my next breath.

"Enough," I growl, flipping us so she's straddling my hips. "I want to watch your face when you take me."

She sinks down slowly, both of us groaning at the exquisite sensation of being joined completely. In this position, with the city lights casting a glow around her like a halo, she looks like a goddess claiming her throne.

"Fuck, you feel incredible," I gasp, my hands gripping her hips.

"So do you," she breathes, starting to move with increasing confidence.

I let her set the pace, watching her face transform with pleasure as she rides me with growing abandon. When she braces her hands on my chest and really starts moving, I nearly lose my mind.

"That's it, sweetheart. Take what you need from me."

Our climax builds slowly, intensely, until we're both trembling on the edge. When she leans down to kiss me, changing the angle in a way that makes us both gasp, I know I'm done for.

"Come with me," I demand, one hand finding her clit while the other tangles in her hair. "I want to feel you fall apart around me."

She shatters with a cry that echoes through my penthouse, and the sensation of her coming triggers my own release. We climax together, maintaining eye contact as waves of pleasure crash over us both.

Afterward, we collapse in a tangle of satisfied limbs, her head pillowed on my chest while I stroke her hair.

"Better?" I ask softly.

"Much better. Though I still think we need to discuss Lauren's interference more seriously."

"There's nothing to discuss. She's part of my past, and a toxic part at that. You're my present and my future, assuming you're brave enough to handle dating someone as obsessed with you as I am."

She traces patterns on my chest, her touch gentle and possessive. "I want to try. The whole terrifying, wonderful, complicated mess of it."

"Good. Because I'm not letting you go without a fight."

My phone buzzes insistently on the nightstand, but I ignore it in favor of holding the woman who's completely scrambled my priorities.

Then it buzzes again. And again.

"You should check that," Rachel says reluctantly.

I grab the phone, seeing multiple urgent texts from Julian. My blood turns to ice as I read them.

"What's wrong?" Rachel asks, sitting up when she sees my expression.

"Hunter Vale's been spreading rumors. Claims your success tonight was bought and paid for, that you're just sleeping your way to artistic recognition."

Chapter 13
Rachel

My phone's been buzzing like a vibrator on steroids for the past hour, and every notification makes my stomach clench tighter. Hunter Vale's poison is spreading through Manhattan's art scene faster than chlamydia at a college frat party.

"Jesus fucking Christ," I mutter, scrolling through Instagram comments that make me want to bleach my eyeballs. "'Talentless whore riding rich dick to success'—well, that's creative. 'Gallery pussy getting what she deserves'—charming. Oh, and my personal favorite: 'Foster trash thinking she can buy class with spread legs.'"

Xander's arm tightens around me where we're sprawled across his stupidly expensive couch. "Don't read that shit. It's digital garbage from people whose biggest accomplishment is spelling their own names correctly."

"But what if they're right? What if everyone thinks my success is just elaborate prostitution?"

"Then everyone's a fucking moron who wouldn't recognize genuine talent if it bit them on their pretentious asses."

THE BILLIONAIRE'S MISTAKEN VOW

Before I can spiral deeper into self-doubt, my apartment buzzer practically screams through the intercom. Peyton's voice crackles through the speaker like an avenging angel with a foul mouth.

"Open up, bitches! I've got emergency coffee and a battle plan!"

Ten minutes later, she's sprawled across Xander's designer furniture like she owns the place, balancing three cups of coffee.

"Okay, let's address the elephant cock in the room," she announces, fixing Xander with her most serious expression. "How massive is your dick, and is it really magical enough to transform struggling artists into successful ones overnight?"

Xander nearly chokes on his coffee. "I'm sorry, what?"

"Peyton, for fuck's sake—" I start.

"No, this is important! Because according to Hunter Vale and his merry band of jealous dickweasels, your penis is apparently some kind of artistic enhancement device. I need to know if I should start sleeping with billionaires to improve my graphic design skills."

"My cock, while admittedly impressive, has no supernatural artistic properties," Xander replies with complete seriousness. "Rachel's success stems entirely from her exceptional talent and years of dedicated practice."

"Damn. There go my get-rich-quick schemes." Peyton turns to me with mock disappointment. "Guess you're just naturally gifted instead of magically dick-enhanced. How boring."

Despite everything, I burst out laughing. "I hate you so much."

"You love me. Besides, someone needs to keep your neurotic ass grounded while these jealous turds try to tear you down." She settles deeper into the couch cushions. "Now, let's discuss strategy. Hunter Vale's been spreading rumors because he's bitter that his pseudo-intellectual bullshit doesn't sell while your emotional honesty does. Classic case of artistic blue balls."

My phone rings before I can respond. Julian's name flashes across the screen with enough urgency to suggest apocalyptic scenarios.

"Rachel, we need an emergency meeting. Now." His voice is tight with stress. "Hunter's been calling collectors, journalists, anyone who'll listen. He's claiming your exhibition sales were orchestrated to inflate your market value artificially."

"Shit. How bad is it?"

"Bad enough that three collectors are requesting authentication of your sales records. They want to verify that the purchases were genuine rather than manufactured hype."

Xander's expression turns murderous. "Those fucking—"

"I'll be there in twenty," I interrupt before he can start planning Hunter's professional execution.

"Actually, bring Xander. This affects his investment too, and we need a unified response."

The gallery feels different when we arrive—charged with tension instead of creative energy. Julian paces behind his desk like a caged predator while Christina examines her manicured nails with studied calm.

THE BILLIONAIRE'S MISTAKEN VOW

"Alright, damage assessment," Julian begins without preamble. "Hunter's convinced three major publications that your relationship with Xander constitutes a conflict of interest that invalidates your artistic credibility."

"That's the stupidest fucking logic I've ever heard," I snap. "Since when do artists need to be celibate to create valid work?"

"Since jealous mediocrity decided to weaponize misogyny," Christina adds dryly. "Though I have to admit, Hunter's strategic about his timing. Your exhibition's success makes the accusations more newsworthy."

Xander's been silent during this exchange, but I can practically see the gears turning behind his ice-blue eyes. When he finally speaks, his voice carries deadly quiet authority.

"Gael's been investigating Hunter's financials. Turns out someone just cleaned up Hunter's back rent and financial mess. Care to guess who?"

My stomach drops like I've been shoved off a cliff. "Lauren."

"Lauren fucking Ashford," he confirms, pulling out his phone. "She's been bankrolling his petty revenge campaign, probably hoping to drive a wedge between us by destroying your reputation."

"That manipulative bitch," Christina breathes with genuine admiration. "I have to respect the tactical sophistication, even while wanting to murder her slowly with a rusty spoon."

Julian runs his hands through his perfectly styled hair, destroying the careful arrangement. "This is exactly what I was afraid of. Personal drama affecting professional reputations, legitimate business relationships being questioned—"

"Then maybe you should've minded your own fucking business instead of playing protective big brother," I interrupt, my temper finally snapping. "I'm a grown woman capable of making my own decisions about my career and my love life."

"Are you? Because from where I'm sitting, dating Xander has made you a target of exactly the kind of sabotage I warned you about."

"And avoiding relationships would've protected me how? By ensuring I remained safely invisible and unsuccessful?"

"That's not what I meant—"

"It's exactly what you meant. Keep little Rachel small and grateful instead of letting her reach for something extraordinary."

The argument might've escalated into something nuclear, but Christina's phone starts buzzing with the persistence of a horny teenager.

"Art world gossip hotline," she answers with professional brightness before her expression shifts to genuine concern. "When did this happen? Are you certain? Fuck. Yes, I'll handle it."

She hangs up.

"That was Damon Wellington. Apparently, Hunter's been making calls suggesting Xander's investment was designed to manipulate the market rather than support genuine talent. Three collectors are now questioning whether they overpaid for artificially inflated work."

The room falls silent except for the sound of my world potentially crashing down around my ears.

"I need to fix this," I say finally, straightening my spine with determination that surprises everyone including myself. "Not through damage control or public relations bullshit. Through work. Real work that proves my talent exists independent of Xander's support."

"How?" Julian asks skeptically.

"By accepting every challenging commission, every difficult exhibition opportunity, every chance to prove myself without Xander's financial backing." I turn to face my billionaire boyfriend, whose expression has shifted from protective fury to reluctant admiration. "I need to do this alone. Publicly, professionally alone."

"Absolutely not," Xander says immediately. "I'm not abandoning you to face this shit storm without support."

"I'm not asking you to abandon me. I'm asking you to let me fight for my own credibility while you handle Lauren and Hunter behind the scenes."

"That's the stupidest plan I've ever heard," Peyton declares from her position sprawled across Julian's desk chair. "You're basically suggesting artistic martyrdom to prove you're not a gold-digging whore."

"Got a better suggestion?"

"Yeah. Fuck what people think and create art so incredible it makes their heads explode with jealous rage. Let your work speak louder than their petty accusations."

Before anyone can respond, Christina's phone buzzes again. Her expression shifts from concern to something approaching panic.

"That was the Whitney. They're hosting a group exhibition next week featuring emerging contemporary artists, and Hunter just convinced them to include a piece addressing 'the commercialization of artistic integrity.' He's planning to make a public statement questioning your legitimacy in front of every major collector and critic in the city."

"Son of a bitch," Xander growls, already reaching for his phone. "I'm calling my lawyers—"

"No." I grab his wrist, stopping him mid-dial. "This is exactly what I was talking about. Let me handle this my way."

"By walking into an ambush?"

"By showing up with new work that'll make Hunter's petty jealousy look exactly as pathetic as it is." I square my shoulders, feeling something fierce and determined crystallizing in my chest. "I'm done hiding from this fight. Time to remind everyone why I belong in this world."

Three days later, I'm standing in the Whitney's pristine white space, watching visitors examine my latest piece—a raw, brutal exploration of how creativity survives despite attempts to diminish it. The painting practically vibrates with angry energy, bold reds and jagged blacks that seem to move under the gallery lights.

Hunter's piece hangs directly across from mine, a pretentious mixed-media installation about "authentic artistic struggle" that looks like someone vomited philosophy textbooks onto canvas.

I'm studying the contrast when his voice cuts through the sophisticated murmur of opening night conversations.

"Well, if it isn't Manhattan's newest artistic prostitute."

Every head in the immediate vicinity turns toward us like we're dinner theater. Hunter stands behind me wearing his trademark smirk and an outfit that screams "tortured artist" louder than a bad indie film.

"Hunter," I acknowledge calmly, not turning around. "Still creating art that explains itself because the visual impact isn't sufficient?"

His smile falters slightly. "At least my work comes from genuine struggle rather than designer bedsheets and billionaire guilt money."

The surrounding conversations halt completely.

Chapter 14
Xander

Watching Rachel face down Hunter Vale in front of Manhattan's art elite is like witnessing a gladiator discover she was born for the arena.

"Interesting perspective," she says, her voice steady as surgical steel. "Though I'm curious—when did financial struggle become a prerequisite for artistic authenticity? Should we discount Picasso because he died wealthy? Dismiss Warhol for his commercial success?"

Hunter's smirk wavers slightly. "That's completely different—"

"Is it? Or are you suggesting that artists, particularly female artists, should remain poor and grateful to validate their creative legitimacy?" She steps closer, her voice carrying clearly through the gallery. "Because that sounds less like artistic integrity and more like internalized misogyny disguised as creative philosophy."

Holy fucking hell. She's not just defending herself—she's dismantling his entire argument.

"You're twisting my words," Hunter protests, but his confidence is visibly cracking.

"Am I? Because your central thesis seems to be that my relationship invalidates my artistic credibility. By that logic, Georgia O'Keeffe's marriage to Alfred Stieglitz should diminish her contributions to American art. Frida Kahlo's partnership with Diego Rivera should overshadow her revolutionary work."

A distinguished woman I recognize as the Metropolitan Museum's contemporary curator nods approvingly. Several other industry professionals exchange impressed glances.

"That's not the same thing," Hunter insists desperately. "You're sleeping with your investor—"

"And you're accepting money from Lauren Ashford to fund this character assassination," Rachel cuts him off with deadly calm. "Should we discuss which arrangement compromises artistic integrity more thoroughly?"

The surrounding crowd inhales collectively. Hunter's face drains of color faster than spilled paint on canvas.

"I don't know what you're talking about," he stammers.

"Don't you? Because I have documentation of payments from Ashford Holdings to your studio account. Back rent and bills all just paid by Lauren, all coincidentally timed with your public campaign against my exhibition success."

She's fucking magnificent. Lethal and brilliant and completely in control of a situation that could've destroyed her reputation permanently.

Gael appears at my elbow, his expression mixing admiration with professional respect. "Your girl's got titanium ovaries," he murmurs.

"She just turned a public execution into a masterclass on intellectual warfare."

"She's incredible," I agree, unable to look away from her commanding presence.

"Also, incredibly independent. Think she needs your white knight routine right now?"

He's right, and I hate him for it. Every protective instinct I possess is screaming to intervene, to use my influence to crush Hunter and Lauren simultaneously. But Rachel's handling this better than I could've imagined.

Hunter retreats like the coward he is, disappearing into the crowd while whispered conversations buzz with new respect for the artist who just eviscerated his credibility with pure intellect.

"That was extraordinary," the Met curator approaches Rachel directly. "I'm Sarah Chen, and I'd love to discuss featuring your work in our upcoming exhibition on emotional expressionism."

"Dr. Martinez, MoMA's acquisition committee," another voice joins in. "Your articulation of artistic authenticity versus commercial success was brilliant. We should schedule a studio visit."

Julian appears beside me, his expression conflicted. "I owe her an apology," he admits quietly. "I thought she needed protection, but she's tougher than both of us combined."

"She's always been tough. We just underestimated her because she's also vulnerable."

"Xander," Julian's voice turns serious. "We need to discuss Lauren's involvement in this clusterfuck. Her funding Hunter crosses lines that could affect gallery business beyond personal drama."

Before I can respond, my phone buzzes with an urgent text from my security team: *Lauren Ashford entering building. VIP elevator, heading to penthouse level.*

"Fuck," I mutter. "Lauren's making a move."

I catch Rachel's eye across the room, mouthing "I'll be back" before heading toward the elevator. If Lauren thinks she can manipulate this situation further, she's about to learn exactly why crossing me professionally is career suicide.

Twenty minutes later, I'm standing in my penthouse facing the woman who spent eighteen months convincing me that love required changing everything about myself to meet her expectations.

"You look well," Lauren says, settling gracefully onto my couch like she still belongs here. "Though I'm concerned about these rumors linking you to that gallery assistant."

"Cut the shit, Lauren. I know you've been bankrolling Hunter's harassment campaign."

Her mask of innocent concern slips slightly. "I don't know what you mean."

"Ashford Holdings, account number ending in 4792, this week's deposits alone totaled fifteen thousand dollars to Hunter Vale's studio account." I pour myself whiskey, not offering her any. "Want me to continue with transaction details, or are we done pretending?"

She sighs delicately, like I'm being unreasonably difficult. "Fine. Yes, I provided some financial assistance to a struggling artist. Is that so terrible?"

"When that assistance funds a targeted campaign to destroy my girlfriend's reputation? Absolutely fucking terrible."

"Girlfriend?" She laughs, the sound brittle as breaking glass. "Xander, darling, she's a rebound. A temporary fascination with someone completely inappropriate for your world."

"She's the woman I'm in love with. The difference between fascination and love is something you never understood."

Lauren's composure cracks entirely. "Love? You never said you loved me, not even after eighteen months of building a life together!"

"Because I didn't. I thought I needed someone who fit seamlessly into my existing world instead of someone who made me want to build a better one."

"You're making a mistake," she whispers, tears threatening her perfect makeup. "She'll leave you the moment someone younger and richer comes along. I know her type—"

"You know nothing about her type because you've never met anyone like her. Rachel creates beauty from pain, fights for what she believes in, and challenges me to be better than I thought possible." I set down my whiskey, fixing her with my coldest stare. "She's everything you pretended to be but never were."

"This isn't over," Lauren says, standing with wounded dignity.

"Yes, it is. Because if you continue interfering with my relationship or Rachel's career, I'll destroy you financially and socially. Your family's foundation, your PR business, your carefully cultivated reputation—all of it disappears."

She pales, finally understanding that eighteen months of intimate knowledge works both ways.

"You wouldn't—"

"Try me. Test whether I care more about past familiarity or protecting the woman I love."

After she leaves, I return to the Whitney to find Rachel surrounded by admirers, business cards accumulating in her hands like trophies. She's glowing with confidence, completely transformed from the nervous artist who worried about belonging in this world.

"How'd it go with Lauren?" she asks when I reach her side.

"Handled. She won't be a problem anymore."

"Good. Because I just accepted three exhibition invitations and two commission offers." Her smile could power half of Manhattan. "Turns out defending my artistic integrity publicly was better marketing than any gallery opening."

"You were fucking incredible," I tell her honestly. "Watching you dismantle Hunter's arguments was the sexiest thing I've ever witnessed."

"Sexier than the time I let you fuck me against my easel?"

"Debatable. We should probably conduct further research."

Her laugh is pure joy, uninhibited and gorgeous. "I love that plan."

We're heading toward the exit when my phone buzzes with a text from an unknown number. The message contains a single photo—Rachel and me kissing in the gallery storage room, clearly taken by someone with professional equipment and excellent timing.

The accompanying message is brief: *Page Six runs this tomorrow unless you reconsider certain recent conversations. – L*

Chapter 15
Rachel

I'm staring at my face plastered across Page Six's website while eating cereal that tastes like cardboard and regret. The headline reads: "BILLIONAIRE'S BEDROOM GAMES: EXCLUSIVE PHOTOS INSIDE RAMSEY'S SECRET AFFAIR."

"Holy fucking shitballs," I mutter, clicking through images that make my private moments look like scenes from a low-budget porno. There's Xander and me kissing in the storage room, his hands clearly groping my ass while I'm pressed against him like a horny teenager.

My phone's been buzzing nonstop since sunrise, which is apparently when Satan's minions at gossip rags publish their daily dose of character assassination.

"This is a goddamn nightmare," I tell my empty apartment, because talking to myself has become my newest coping mechanism. "My vagina is now a matter of public record."

The apartment door practically explodes inward as Peyton arrives like a foul-mouthed fairy godmother armed with coffee and righteous fury.

"Alright, bitches, Mama's here to fix this clusterfuck!" she announces, dumping her laptop and three cups of espresso onto my kitchen table.

"I've been up since four AM creating damage control content that'll make these gossip vultures choke on their own bullshit."

"Peyton, you beautiful disaster, how exactly do we fix photos of me getting felt up by Manhattan's most eligible bachelor?"

"Simple. We flood social media with content about your artistic genius until people forget you have functioning reproductive organs." She fires up her laptop with the intensity of a NASA launch sequence. "I've designed graphics highlighting your exhibition sales, quotes from collectors praising your technique, testimonials from art critics who can't spell 'vagina' if their trust funds depended on it."

I peer over her shoulder as she scrolls through professionally designed posts that make my artistic achievements look fucking impressive. "Jesus Christ, when did you become a PR wizard?"

"When my best friend started dating someone whose dick is apparently newsworthy." She grins wickedly. "Besides, I've been designing social campaigns for influencers who've done way worse shit than fall in love with rich guys. Remember that lifestyle blogger who got caught faking her entire personality? This is nothing."

My phone rings, Christina's name appearing like salvation wrapped in designer clothing.

"Darling, have you seen the coverage?" Her voice carries that particular blend of concern and professional calculation that makes her invaluable in crises.

"Unfortunately. I look like a sex-crazed gold digger who fucks her way to artistic success."

"Actually, you look like a gorgeous woman in love with someone who clearly adores you. The problem isn't the photos—it's the narrative spinning around them." Papers rustle in the background. "I've been monitoring coverage across different outlets. The art publications are focusing on your talent, the business journals are analyzing Xander's investment strategy, and only the gossip rags are obsessing over your sex life."

"So basically, people who matter professionally aren't treating this like amateur porn?"

"Exactly. Though we should discuss media training. Xander's PR team wants to arrange interviews where you can control the conversation."

Before I can respond, my phone buzzes with texts from numbers I don't recognize:

Saw your work at the Whitney. Incredible emotional depth. Ignore the gossip bullshit. - Rebecca Martinez, MoMA

Your articulation of artistic authenticity was brilliant. Media circus doesn't diminish your talent. - Sarah Chen, Met

Keep creating. Real artists recognize real art. - David Kim, Guggenheim

"Holy shit," I breathe, reading message after message from established artists and curators. "Christina, people are actually defending me. Like, important people with fancy titles and everything."

"Of course they are. You think anyone who's built a legitimate career in the arts gives a flying fuck about gossip magazine speculation? They care about talent, and you've got it in spades."

Peyton looks up from her laptop, where she's apparently designing what looks like a small advertising empire. "Plus, I've been reaching out to art bloggers and influencers who focus on emerging talent. Half of them are already sharing your work with captions about supporting artists despite media manipulation."

"You beautiful, crude genius. How are you this good at crisis management?"

"Years of watching reality TV and learning from other people's public relations disasters. Also, I may have accidentally minored in marketing because I thought it was an easy A." She shrugs like accidentally acquiring useful skills is totally normal. "Point is, we're shifting the narrative from 'artist fucks billionaire' to 'talented woman succeeds despite media harassment.'"

My apartment door chimes, and Xander's voice carries through the intercom like verbal chocolate.

"It's me. Open up before I murder everyone at Page Six with my bare hands." I turn to Peyton. "Fair warning—he's probably in full protective caveman mode."

"Good. I want to see billionaire rage up close. Bet he's even hotter when he's homicidal."

Xander enters looking like he stepped off the cover of Angry CEO Weekly—perfectly tailored suit, jaw clenched tight enough to crack walnuts, ice-blue eyes promising professional destruction for anyone who crossed him.

"Are you alright?" He cups my face immediately, scanning for damage like someone might've physically injured me through internet gossip.

"I'm fine. Embarrassed as hell, but fine. Peyton's been creating social media magic while Christina coordinates damage control with actual adults."

"My PR team's been fielding interview requests all morning," he says, his thumb stroking my cheek. "We can control this narrative, but it requires us presenting a united front publicly."

"Meaning?"

"Meaning we do a joint interview. Something classy, professional, focused on our shared interests rather than letting gossip rags define our relationship."

Peyton snorts. "Translation: you parade around looking respectable while discussing art and business instead of how amazing the sex is."

"The sex is fucking incredible," Xander replies without missing a beat, "but that's nobody's business except ours."

"I love that you two can discuss your sex life like it's weather patterns," I mutter, pouring more coffee because this conversation requires industrial-strength caffeine.

"Speaking of weather patterns," Christina's voice crackles through my phone speaker, "Xander's team has arranged an interview with Manhattan Arts Quarterly. Very respectable publication, focuses on collectors and cultural philanthropy rather than bedroom athletics."

My stomach lurches. "An interview? Like, on camera? Where people can see my face and judge my words?"

"Where people can see you're articulate, passionate about your work, and genuinely connected to someone who respects your talent," Xander corrects gently. "This is our chance to define the narrative instead of letting others do it for us."

"What if I say something stupid? What if they ask about my background, or whether I'd be successful without your support, or—"

"Then you tell the truth," he interrupts. "That you're an incredible artist who earned every opportunity through talent and hard work. That our relationship enhances your life but doesn't define your worth."

Peyton looks up from her laptop, where she's apparently created an entire social media empire in the past hour. "Plus, I'll be monitoring comments and responses in real time. Anyone posts negative shit, I'll flood their mentions with photographic evidence of your artistic genius."

"You're terrifying and I love you."

"I know. Now, let's discuss what you're wearing for this interview, because if you're going public, you need to look like the artistic goddess you are."

Two hours later, I'm sitting in a makeup chair at Manhattan Arts Quarterly's offices, trying not to hyperventilate while someone transforms my face into television-appropriate perfection.

"You're going to be brilliant," Xander murmurs, his hand finding mine as we wait for the cameras to start rolling.

"What if they ask the wrong questions? What if I freeze up? What if—"

The interviewer, a distinguished woman with kind eyes and expensive hair, settles across from us with her notes.

"Ms. Brooks, Mr. Ramsey, thank you for joining us today. I'd like to start with a simple question." She fixes me with a direct stare that makes my palms sweat. "Ms. Brooks, do you believe you would have achieved your current level of success without Mr. Ramsey's influence and investment?"

Fuck. The exact question I was terrified she'd ask.

Chapter 16
Xander

Watching Rachel face down that interview question is like watching my warrior discover she was born for battle.

She takes a breath that I can see steadying her entire frame, then looks directly into the camera with those gorgeous green eyes blazing with quiet confidence.

"That's an excellent question," she says, her voice clear and unwavering. "The truth is, my art existed long before I met Xander. I've been painting since I was eight years old, working with whatever supplies I could afford or steal from school art rooms. I graduated with honors while working three jobs, and I created the pieces in my exhibition over months of late nights in my cramped studio."

The interviewer leans forward, clearly impressed by her directness.

"Xander's investment provided me with better materials, professional framing, and access to collectors I never could have reached on my own," Rachel continues. "But investment doesn't create talent. It reveals it. The emotions in my paintings, the technique I've developed, the vision that drives my work—those came from years of practice and a desperate need to transform pain into something beautiful."

Fuck me sideways, she's magnificent.

"So, to answer your question directly—yes, I believe I would have achieved success eventually. It might have taken longer, required more struggle, but talent finds a way to surface. Xander didn't make me an artist. He just helped me become the artist I was always meant to be."

The interviewer's smile turns genuinely warm. "That's beautifully articulated. Mr. Ramsey, what drew you to invest in emerging artists rather than established names?"

I squeeze Rachel's hand before answering. "Established art is safe, predictable. It's an asset class, not a passion. But watching someone like Rachel create something that didn't exist five minutes before—that's witnessing actual magic. Her painting about yearning made me understand emotions I didn't even know I had."

"And the personal relationship that developed?"

"Was completely unexpected and entirely separate from my business decision," I reply smoothly. "I invested in her work before our first date. Her talent convinced me she was worth backing. Everything else was just two people discovering they're stupidly compatible."

Rachel snorts quietly at 'stupidly compatible,' and I have to bite back a grin.

"Stupidly compatible," the interviewer repeats with amusement. "Can you elaborate?"

"She challenges every assumption I have about what matters," I explain. "She makes me laugh at inappropriate moments, argues with me about everything from coffee preferences to business ethics, and creates art that makes me question why I ever thought money was more important than beauty."

"That's quite romantic."

"It's quite terrifying," Rachel interjects, making everyone laugh. "Dating someone whose net worth has more zeros than my address zip code requires constant reality checks."

"How do you handle the class differences?"

"By remembering that class is about behavior, not bank accounts," she replies without hesitation. "I've met wealthy people with absolutely no class and poor people who could teach etiquette courses. Xander treats everyone with respect regardless of their financial situation. That matters more than whether he knows which fork to use."

Christ, I'm falling deeper in love with her every second.

After the cameras stop rolling, the interviewer shakes our hands enthusiastically.

"That was refreshing," she says. "Most celebrity couples give canned responses. You two actually like each other."

"We actually do," Rachel grins, and something warm explodes in my chest.

We're heading toward the elevator when my phone buzzes with a text from Gael: *Watching the interview. $500 says you propose within two months. Another $500 says she cries. Final $500 says Julian objects to something during the ceremony.*

I show the message to Rachel, who bursts out laughing.

"Your best friend is placing bets on our hypothetical engagement?"

"Gael places bets on everything. Yesterday he wagered on whether the coffee shop barista would spell his name correctly."

"Did she?"

"She wrote 'Gayle' on his cup. He lost twenty bucks to himself."

Rachel's still giggling when Julian calls, his voice carrying obvious pride through the speaker.

"That was fucking brilliant," he says without preamble. "Both of you handled those questions like seasoned politicians. The gallery's phone has been ringing nonstop with collectors asking about Rachel's future work."

"Really?" Rachel's face lights up like Christmas morning.

"Really. Sarah Chen from the Met wants to schedule a studio visit. Damon Wellington is asking about commission possibilities. Even that pretentious asshole from the Whitney admitted your interview was 'refreshingly authentic.'"

"Holy shit," she breathes.

"Also, Xander, I owe you both an apology. My protective instincts made me act like a condescending prick. Rachel's proven she can handle anything this world throws at her."

"Damn right I can," she declares, then softens. "But I appreciate you caring enough to worry, even if your methods were questionable."

"My methods were shit," Julian admits. "I forgot that strength comes in different forms. Yours just happens to include the ability to eviscerate pompous artists with pure intellect."

Three days later, I'm in my office reviewing Rachel's latest commission requests when Gael strolls in wearing his trademark shit-eating grin.

"So," he announces, settling into the chair across from my desk, "I've been thinking about your girlfriend situation."

"Please don't."

"Too late. I've decided she needs more high-profile opportunities that are clearly merit-based rather than boyfriend-funded."

I pause mid-signature. "What kind of opportunities?"

"The Steinberg Foundation is launching a scholarship program for emerging artists. Completely anonymous selection process, judged by a panel that doesn't know who's dating whom." His expression turns serious. "Rachel's work would qualify easily, and winning would establish her credibility beyond any gossip bullshit."

"That's... actually brilliant."

"I have my moments. I also contacted three gallery owners who've never met either of you. Sent them images of her work without identifying information. All three want to represent her."

"Gael." I'm genuinely moved by his effort to help her succeed independently.

"What? I like her. She makes you less of an uptight control freak, and she laughs at my inappropriate jokes without looking horrified." He grins wickedly. "Plus, watching you fall this hard is entertainment gold. I'm documenting the whole process for future blackmail material."

Before I can threaten his life, my assistant Maria buzzes through the intercom.

"Mr. Ramsey? Lauren Ashford is here to see you. She says it's urgent."

"Send her away."

"She claims you promised to discuss reconciliation before you met Ms. Brooks."

Gael's eyebrows disappear into his hairline. "Oh, this should be good. Want me to stay for the show?"

"Absolutely not. This ends today."

Lauren enters looking like she's dressed for her own funeral—black designer dress, perfect makeup that can't quite hide the desperation in her eyes.

"Xander, darling, we need to talk privately about the promises you made before this infatuation began."

"What promises?" I don't bother standing or offering her a seat.

"You said we had unfinished business. That you needed time to focus on work before we could move forward properly."

"I said our relationship was over and you needed to accept that reality."

"That's not how I remember it."

"Then your memory's conveniently selective." I lean back in my chair, studying her with clinical detachment. "What do you want, Lauren?"

"I want you to remember what we built together. Eighteen months of compatibility, shared goals, mutual understanding—"

"Eighteen months of you trying to reshape me into your ideal accessory while I convinced myself that settling was mature." I stand finally, moving to the window. "I'm in love with someone who makes me want to be better, not different. Someone who challenges me instead of managing me."

"You think she loves you for yourself? She's using you just like I did, except she's better at hiding it."

"No, she's not. Rachel fights me on everything from restaurant choices to business decisions. She pays for her own coffee, refuses expensive gifts, and gets genuinely angry when I try to solve her problems for her." I turn to face Lauren directly. "She's nothing like you, which is exactly why I love her."

Lauren's composure finally cracks completely. "This isn't over. When she leaves you for someone younger or richer, don't come crawling back expecting forgiveness."

"She won't leave. But if she did, I still wouldn't want you back. Some mistakes teach you exactly what you don't want."

After she goes, I sit in my office thinking about grand gestures and perfect timing. Rachel deserves something spectacular, something that shows the entire art world how proud I am to love her.

I'm reaching for my phone to call the jeweler I've been researching when Gael bursts through the door like he's fleeing a crime scene.

"We need to discuss engagement rings immediately," he announces. "I've been researching vintage pieces that match her aesthetic, and holy fuck, some of these diamonds are bigger than my apartment."

"Keep your voice down," I hiss, but it's too late as I see Rachel and her expression tells me she has heard every word.

Chapter 17
Rachel

"Holy fucking Christ, he's buying engagement rings."

I'm sprawled across Peyton's couch at seven in the morning, clutching my third cup of coffee while having what can only be described as a full-scale panic attack about my love life.

"How exactly do you know this?" Peyton asks, examining her chipped black nail polish with studied casualness.

"Because Gael texted me last night asking about my ring size and preferred gemstone cuts. Apparently, Xander's been 'researching vintage pieces that match my aesthetic.'" I make air quotes around the phrase like it's contaminated. "We've been together for barely two months, Peyton. Two fucking months, and he's already planning to propose."

"And this is bad because...?"

"Because I'm not ready! Because marriage is permanent, and permanent things never work out for me. Because what if he realizes I'm just some damaged foster kid who doesn't belong in his world?"

Peyton sets down her coffee and fixes me with her most serious expression. "Rach, when's the last time you let yourself have something good without immediately planning its destruction?"

"That's not what I'm doing."

"Bullshit. You're already convinced he's going to leave, so you're looking for reasons to run first." She curls up in her chair, tucking her legs beneath her. "Let me ask you something - do you love him?"

"That's not the point-"

"Do you fucking love him?"

Heat creeps up my neck. "Yes. Stupidly, completely, terrifyingly in love with him."

"And does he make you happy?"

"When I'm not panicking about our future, yes."

"Does he respect your art, support your career, make you come so hard you forget your own name?"

"Peyton!"

"Answer the question!"

"Yes to all of the above, you crude bitch."

"Then what exactly is the problem? You found a gorgeous billionaire who worships your pussy and treats you like a goddess. Most women would kill for that combination."

I bury my face in a throw pillow. "The problem is I don't know how to be someone's forever person. Everyone leaves eventually. Foster families, social workers, boyfriends who realize I'm too much work."

"Xander's not everyone else," Peyton says gently, her voice losing its usual sarcasm. "He's fought for you publicly, defended your reputation, invested in your career. That's not someone who's planning to bail."

"But what if-"

"What if aliens invade Manhattan and declare war on abstract artists? What if you win the lottery and become so rich you dump him for someone prettier? What if, what if, what if." She throws a pillow at my head. "You can't live your entire life afraid of hypothetical disasters."

Before I can argue further, my phone rings. Christina's name appears like salvation wrapped in designer clothing.

"Darling, I heard through the grapevine that Xander's been jewelry shopping," she says without preamble. "Are we celebrating or staging an intervention?"

"Intervention. Definitely intervention. I'm not ready for this level of commitment."

"Honey, you realize that Xander Ramsey doesn't casually browse engagement rings, right? He's not the type for grand romantic gestures unless he's absolutely certain about someone."

I switch to speaker so Peyton can hear. "That's what scares me. What if I disappoint him? What if I'm not sophisticated enough to be someone's wife?"

"First of all, marriage isn't about sophistication - it's about finding someone who makes you want to be better while loving you exactly as you are. Second, Xander's not proposing to impress his social circle.

He's proposing because you've made him happier than I've ever seen him."

"How can you be sure?"

"Because I've watched him date for years. Those other women got expensive jewelry, sure, but it was always transaction-based. Buy her something pretty, keep her happy, maintain the relationship status quo." Christina's voice turns thoughtful. "With you, he's planning something meaningful. Something that represents your shared story rather than his bank account."

The distinction hits me harder than expected. "You think he's serious about building a life together?"

"I think he's ready to make you a permanent part of his world, which is terrifying and wonderful and exactly what you both need."

Two hours later, I'm standing outside Xander's office building, my stomach performing gymnastic routines that would impress Olympic judges. His assistant Maria waves me toward the elevator with a knowing smile.

"He's expecting you," she says warmly. "Conference room's empty if you need privacy for whatever conversation's got you looking like you're about to commit homicide."

Xander's office door is open, and I find him bent over architectural plans, his sleeves rolled up to reveal those forearms that make my brain malfunction. He looks up when I enter, his face lighting up with genuine pleasure.

"This is a nice surprise," he says, standing to kiss me hello. "Though you look like you're about to deliver terrible news."

"We need to discuss your apparent engagement ring shopping," I blurt out.

He freezes mid-kiss. "My what?"

"Gael texted me about ring sizes. You've been researching vintage pieces. The whole office probably knows you're planning to propose."

His expression shifts through several emotions before settling on resigned amusement. "I'm going to murder my best friend with my bare hands."

"So, it's true?"

"It's complicated." He runs a hand through his perfectly styled hair, destroying the careful arrangement. "Yes, I've been looking at rings. No, I don't have immediate proposal plans. I wanted to be prepared when the timing felt right."

"When would that be? Because two months seems incredibly fast for someone who's never been married."

"When you stop looking terrified every time someone mentions our future together," he replies honestly. "When you believe that I'm not going anywhere regardless of what the media says or your background suggests."

His directness catches me off guard. "I'm not terrified."

"You're absolutely terrified. And that's okay, because frankly, so am I."

"You're scared of marrying me?"

"I'm scared of fucking this up. Of moving too fast and pushing you away. Of not moving fast enough and losing you to someone who doesn't come with my baggage." He moves closer, his hands framing my face. "I'm scared that eighteen months with Lauren convinced me I don't know how relationships work with someone I actually love."

The raw honesty in his voice makes my chest tight. "What if we're both disasters at this?"

"Then we'll be disasters together. But Rachel, I need you to understand something." His thumbs brush across my cheekbones. "I'm not proposing because society expects it or because it looks good for business. I'm thinking about it because I can't imagine my future without you in it."

"Even if I never fit perfectly into your world?"

"Especially if you never fit perfectly. I don't want someone who fits - I want someone who makes me question why that world matters."

Before I can overthink his response, I'm kissing him with desperate hunger, months of emotion exploding between us. He tastes like coffee and possibility, and when he groans against my mouth, rational thought abandons me entirely.

"Lock the door," I whisper against his lips.

"Rachel-"

"Lock the fucking door, Xander."

He complies without argument, and suddenly I'm pushing him toward the leather couch in his office's seating area, my hands already working at his shirt buttons.

"Here? Now?" he asks, but his voice is rough with desire.

"Here. Now. Before I lose my nerve about everything." I straddle his lap, feeling his immediate response through expensive fabric. "I need to show you something."

"What?"

"How much I want this. Want you. Want us, even if it scares the shit out of me."

I grind against him slowly, watching his control slip as his hands grip my hips. The way he looks at me - like I'm the answer to every question he's ever had - makes heat pool low in my belly.

"Christ, you're incredible," he breathes, his hands sliding beneath my dress.

"I love you," I tell him, the words coming easier now. "I love you enough to be terrified of losing you."

"You're not going to lose me." His fingers find the edge of my panties, and I gasp. "I'm not going anywhere, sweetheart."

I stand long enough to strip out of my dress and underwear, watching his eyes darken as he takes in my naked body. When I reach for his belt, his hands cover mine.

"Are you sure about this? Here?"

"I've never been more sure of anything." I free him from his pants, stroking him slowly. "I want to feel how much you need me."

"Fuck, Rachel." His head falls back as I work him with gentle touches. "I need you more than breathing."

I position myself above him, sinking down slowly until we're completely joined. The sensation makes us both groan, and for a moment we just stay like that, foreheads pressed together.

"This feels like claiming," I whisper, starting to move.

"It is claiming." His hands guide my hips, helping me find the perfect rhythm. "You're mine, and I'm yours, and I don't give a damn who knows it."

I ride him slowly, deliberately, maintaining eye contact as pleasure builds between us. "I'm scared of forever," I confess breathlessly.

"So am I," he admits, his voice strained. "But I'm more scared of a future without you in it."

"What if I'm not wife material?"

"What if you're exactly the wife material I need?" His thumb finds my clit, circling with perfect pressure. "What if we're both overthinking this?"

"Jesus, don't stop doing that," I gasp, my movements becoming more desperate.

"Never stopping. Never leaving. Never giving up on us." Each word is punctuated by his touch, driving me closer to the edge. "I love watching you fall apart for me."

"Xander, I'm going to-"

"Come for me, baby. Let me feel how good I make you feel."

My orgasm crashes over me like a tidal wave, and I cry out his name as pleasure floods every nerve ending. The sensation of me climaxing triggers his own release, and he buries himself deep as he comes with a groan that echoes through his office.

We collapse together, breathing heavily as aftershocks pulse between us. I rest my head on his shoulder, feeling more settled than I have in weeks.

"Better?" he asks softly, stroking my hair.

"Much better. Though your assistant probably heard us."

"Maria's been married for thirty years. She understands passion."

I lift my head to look at him. "So, about this ring shopping..."

"We'll take it as slow as you need. No pressure, no timeline, just us figuring it out together."

"And if I'm never ready for marriage?"

"Then we'll find other ways to build a life together. But Rachel?" He cups my face gently. "I think you're braver than you know. And I think you want forever as much as I do, even if the idea terrifies you."

Before I can respond, his phone starts buzzing insistently on his desk. Julian's name flashes repeatedly across the screen.

"You should answer that," I say reluctantly, climbing off his lap to find my clothes.

Xander grabs the phone, putting it on speaker while he straightens his tie. "This better be important, Julian."

"Hunter's been arrested," Julian's voice cuts through the post-orgasmic haze like a blade. "He vandalized three of Rachel's pieces at the Tribeca Contemporary gallery. Security footage shows him pouring paint stripper across the canvases."

Chapter 18
Xander

The urge to hunt Hunter Vale down and break his fingers one by one is so overwhelming I have to grip my desk edge to keep from walking out of this office and committing multiple felonies.

"How bad is the damage?" I ask Julian, though my voice sounds like it's coming from someone else entirely.

"Three pieces completely destroyed. Paint stripper ate through the canvas, the frames are warped, and the bastard spray-painted 'FAKE WHORE' across what's left of the Yearning landscape."

White-hot rage explodes behind my eyes. That painting—the one that made me understand what real art could do to someone's soul—is gone. Destroyed by some jealous prick who couldn't handle Rachel's talent outshining his mediocre bullshit.

Rachel's gone completely still beside me, her face pale as marble.

"Insurance will cover the monetary value," Julian continues, "but obviously there's no replacing the actual artwork. The gallery's devastated. These pieces were supposed to anchor next month's emerging artists showcase."

"I'm going to destroy him," I say quietly, my voice deadly calm. "Professionally, financially, socially—I'm going to erase Hunter Vale from existence."

"Xander, no." Rachel's hand touches my arm, her voice steady despite the shock. "Don't make this about revenge. Make it about justice."

"Same fucking thing in this case."

"No, it's not." She straightens her shoulders, and I watch her transform from vulnerable woman to fierce warrior right before my eyes. "Revenge is what weak people do when they can't create anything worthwhile themselves. Justice is letting the legal system handle his criminal behavior while I prove my work speaks louder than his vandalism."

Christ, she's magnificent even when she's been wounded.

"Besides," she continues, "if you go nuclear on Hunter, the media will say I need my billionaire boyfriend to fight my battles. I'd rather handle this myself."

Before I can argue that point, my office door practically explodes inward as Gael arrives looking like he's been conducting surveillance operations all morning.

"Holy fuck, have you seen the security footage?" He waves his phone like evidence in a murder trial. "Hunter Vale creeping around the gallery at three AM with industrial paint stripper and daddy issues. It's like watching artistic terrorism in real time."

"How did you get security footage?" I demand.

"I have connections everywhere, including gallery security systems." His grin turns predatory. "Also, I've been monitoring his financial records since this whole clusterfuck started. Want to guess who's been funding his art supplies and therapy sessions?"

"Lauren," Rachel and I say simultaneously.

"Lauren fucking Ashford, paying for this psychopath's rampage while probably hoping it would drive you two apart." Gael settles into my office chair like he owns the place. "Though I have to say, Hunter's complete mental breakdown makes for fascinating psychological theater. The man's basically having an artistic tantrum because his penis substitute paintings can't compete with actual emotional depth."

"Jesus Christ, Gael," I mutter.

"What? I'm being supportive! Rachel's work triggers genuine human feelings, while Hunter creates pretentious garbage that looks like someone vomited philosophy textbooks onto canvas. Of course he's having a breakdown."

Despite everything, Rachel snorts with laughter. "That's actually the most accurate description of his art I've ever heard."

"I live to serve. Also, I've been researching his psychological profile, and this escalation pattern suggests serious instability." Gael's expression turns unusually serious. "Vandalism today, potential violence tomorrow. We need to consider personal security for Rachel."

"Already handled," I tell him, pulling up my security team's report. "Twenty-four-hour protection, tracking on Hunter's movements, and a restraining order being filed within the hour."

"Good, because the man's apparently been writing manifesto-style rants about artistic purity and the corruption of genuine talent by commercial influence." Gael shows us screenshots that make my blood run cold. "Sample quote: 'The whore and her billionaire will learn that real art can't be bought or sold, only destroyed and reborn through cleansing fire.'"

"He's completely lost his shit," Rachel breathes, reading over the disturbing text.

"Completely. Though on the bright side, his public meltdown is generating massive sympathy for you. Art critics are calling this an attack on creative freedom, collectors are expressing outrage at the destruction of emerging talent, and apparently the Met wants to fast-track your next exhibition as a statement against artistic terrorism."

My phone buzzes with a call from Julian, his voice tight with stress when I answer.

"Xander, we need to discuss gallery security upgrades immediately. I should have recognized Hunter's behavior was escalating beyond normal jealousy."

"What do you mean?" Rachel asks.

"He'd been hanging around the galleries where you showed, asking pointed questions about your sales, your relationship with Xander, whether the purchases were legitimate." Julian's guilt bleeds through the speaker. "I thought it was typical artist rivalry, not genuine stalking behavior."

"Don't blame yourself," Rachel says firmly. "Hunter's choices are his own responsibility."

"Still, I should have been more protective. You're family, Rachel, and I failed to keep you safe."

The genuine emotion in my brother's voice hits me unexpectedly. Despite our complicated history, Julian truly cares about Rachel's wellbeing.

"We all missed the signs," I tell him. "Focus on moving forward—better security, legal consequences, and making sure this shit never happens again."

"Already implementing new protocols. Motion sensors, upgraded cameras, security guards during evening hours. The other artists are spooked, but they're also rallying around Rachel."

"How so?"

"Social media campaigns supporting her work, statements condemning Hunter's vandalism, offers to donate pieces for a rebuild exhibition." Julian's voice warms slightly. "The art community doesn't tolerate attacks on emerging talent, especially not gender-based harassment disguised as artistic criticism."

Gael looks up from his phone, where he's been monitoring media coverage. "Speaking of community support, Rachel's about to become the poster child for persevering through artistic adversity. Three major publications want interviews, collectors are specifically requesting her work, and someone started a hashtag—#ArtSurvivesVandalism—that's trending nationally."

"I don't want to be a poster child," Rachel protests. "I want to be an artist."

"You can be both," I tell her, stroking her hair gently. "Use the attention to showcase your talent, then let the work speak for itself."

"Easy for you to say. You're not the one whose personal trauma is about to become public entertainment."

She's right, and the thought of media vultures picking apart her foster care background makes me want to commit violence against several journalists.

"My legal team can control the narrative," I offer. "Limit interviews to art-focused publications, require approval of all questions, maintain your privacy while still capitalizing on the support."

"That could work," she admits reluctantly. "Though I still think this is insane. Six months ago I was eating ramen and painting in my shitty apartment. Now I'm apparently the face of artistic resilience?"

"Now you're a talented woman who refused to be intimidated by jealous mediocrity," I correct. "The universe has a weird sense of timing, but your success isn't accidental."

My phone buzzes with another call—this time from my head of security, Vincent.

"Sir, we've located Hunter Vale. He's barricaded himself in his studio and is refusing to cooperate with police. Initial reports suggest he's destroying his own artwork and ranting about purification through fire."

"Is he armed?"

"Unknown. NYPD has the building surrounded, but they're treating this as a potential mental health crisis rather than standard arrest protocol."

Rachel's face goes white. "He's having a complete breakdown."

"Good," Gael says without sympathy. "Maybe now people will recognize he's been unhinged all along instead of treating his harassment as legitimate artistic discourse."

"Gael, the man clearly needs psychiatric help," Rachel protests.

"The man clearly needs to face consequences for criminal behavior," I counter. "Mental health issues don't excuse vandalism, stalking, or terroristic threats."

Before the argument can escalate, Vincent calls back with updates.

"Sir, Hunter's been taken into custody. No weapons found, but his studio was completely destroyed—he'd been systematically burning his own paintings while documenting the process. Preliminary psychiatric evaluation suggests acute psychotic episode triggered by perceived professional failure."

"And Lauren's involvement?" I ask.

"Financial records confirm she's been funding his living expenses for three months. We have documented transfers totaling forty-three thousand dollars, plus evidence of coordinated communication about targeting Ms. Brooks' reputation."

Perfect. Now I have leverage against both of them.

"Rachel," I turn to face her directly, "I need you to understand something. Hunter's breakdown gives us legal ammunition, but Lauren's orchestration makes this a conspiracy. I can ensure both face maximum consequences, but only if you're comfortable with the exposure that comes with pressing charges."

She considers this, her green eyes thoughtful. "What kind of exposure?"

"Court proceedings, media coverage, detailed examination of everything they've done to sabotage your career." I cup her face gently. "It means your foster care background becomes public record, our relationship gets dissected legally, and Lauren's manipulation tactics become headline news."

"Will it stop them from trying this shit again?"

"Permanently."

She nods decisively. "Then let's fucking do it. I'm tired of running from fights I didn't start."

Gael grins wickedly. "This is going to be spectacular. Lauren Ashford's trust fund reputation getting destroyed in open court while Hunter Vale's artistic pretensions get exposed as jealous psychosis? I'm clearing my calendar to watch this legal bloodbath."

"It's not entertainment," I warn him.

"Everything's entertainment when justice involves destroying people who attacked someone I care about." His expression turns serious. "Rachel's good for you, Xander. Anyone who can't see that deserves whatever legal hell you unleash."

As we're finalizing strategy, my phone buzzes with an encrypted message from my private intelligence firm: *L. Ashford planning final move. Source indicates charity auction next week. Private foster records obtained through illegal channels. Full exposure planned for maximum social damage.*

Chapter 19
Rachel

"Holy fucking Christ, I look like a goddamn princess who stumbled into the wrong fairy tale," I mutter, staring at my reflection in Christina's full-length mirror.

The midnight blue gown she selected transforms me into someone I barely recognize—silk that flows like liquid starlight, a neckline that suggests rather than screams, and a silhouette that makes my curves look intentional instead of accidental.

"You look like a woman who belongs anywhere she damn well pleases," Peyton declares from her sprawled position across Christina's designer couch. "Xander's going to take one look at you and forget his own goddamn name."

"More importantly," Christina adds, fastening a delicate diamond necklace around my throat, "you look like someone whose art deserves to hang beside Picassos and Pollocks."

My stomach performs Olympic-level gymnastics at the reminder. Tonight, my piece will be auctioned alongside works by masters whose names appear in art history textbooks. People with more money than small countries will bid on something I created in my cramped Queens studio.

"What if nobody bids?" I whisper, the fear I've been suppressing finally escaping.

"Then I'll bid myself into bankruptcy just to watch you succeed," Peyton says fiercely. "Though honestly, if these rich assholes don't recognize genius when they see it, they deserve to have their trust funds revoked."

Christina's phone buzzes with updates from the auction venue. "Initial preview responses are exceptional. Your emotional landscape piece is generating significant interest among serious collectors."

"Really?"

"Really. Damon Wellington called it 'devastatingly beautiful,' and Sarah Chen from the Met used the phrase 'raw authenticity' approximately seventeen times." Christina's smile could power Manhattan. "You're about to become very wealthy, darling."

An hour later, I'm walking into the Plaza's Grand Ballroom on Xander's arm, trying not to hyperventilate at the sheer opulence surrounding us. Crystal chandeliers cast golden light over Manhattan's elite, their jewelry probably worth more than most people's houses.

"Breathe, sweetheart," Xander murmurs against my ear, his hand steady at the small of my back. "You belong here as much as anyone else."

"Easy for you to say. You were born into this world."

"I was born into money. You were born with talent. Which matters more?"

Before I can answer, a distinguished gentleman approaches with obvious enthusiasm.

"Ms. Brooks! Jonathan Hartwell, Hartwell Foundation. Your piece is absolutely extraordinary—such emotional depth and technical sophistication."

"Thank you," I manage, falling into the polite conversation patterns Christina drilled into me.

"I understand you're self-taught? Remarkable. Raw talent refined through pure determination is increasingly rare in today's commercial art world."

The conversation flows easier than expected, and gradually I realize these people genuinely appreciate artistic ability over social pedigree. My background becomes an asset rather than liability—proof of dedication that privileged artists might never develop.

"Excuse me, Ms. Brooks."

I turn to find Lauren Ashford approaching like a designer-clad shark, her smile sharp enough to perform surgery. My blood turns to ice water, but I keep my expression neutral.

"Lauren," I acknowledge evenly.

"I couldn't help overhearing your conversation about artistic backgrounds. So fascinating how childhood experiences shape creative expression." Her voice drips false sweetness. "I imagine growing up in foster care provided unique inspiration for your emotional landscapes."

The surrounding conversations pause slightly. She's trying to embarrass me publicly, make my past sound like something shameful that disqualifies me from this world.

"It absolutely did," I reply clearly, my voice carrying to nearby listeners. "Learning early that homes are temporary teaches you to find stability in creation rather than circumstance. Every placement taught me different perspectives on family, belonging, and resilience."

Lauren's smile falters as I continue.

"Foster care showed me that worth isn't determined by birth circumstances but by how you choose to grow despite challenges. Some of my most powerful pieces explore themes of impermanence and hope—emotions I understand intimately because I lived them."

"How admirably you've overcome such difficult origins," Lauren says, but her tone suggests the opposite.

"I haven't overcome them—I've transformed them into strength. The vulnerability required for honest art comes from experiencing genuine loss and learning to trust again." I step closer, lowering my voice. "Something people born into guaranteed security might struggle to access."

Jonathan Hartwell nods approvingly. "Authentic emotional experience creates authentic art. Your work resonates because it comes from lived truth rather than theoretical understanding."

Lauren retreats like the coward she is, her attempt at public humiliation backfiring spectacularly. Several other donors approach with genuine interest in my background and artistic journey.

"Brilliantly handled," Xander whispers when we have a moment alone. "You turned her weapon into armor."

"I'm tired of being ashamed of surviving difficult circumstances. My past made me who I am—someone who creates beauty from pain."

"And I'm fucking proud of who you are," he says, his voice rough with emotion.

The auction begins with traditional pieces—a small Monet, some contemporary sculptures, established artists whose work sells for predictable amounts. Then the auctioneer announces my piece.

"Lot forty-seven: 'Yearning 2' by emerging artist Rachel Brooks. Oil on canvas, exploring themes of longing and emotional transformation. We'll start bidding at ten thousand dollars."

My heart pounds as hands raise around the room. Ten becomes fifteen, then twenty-five, then forty. The numbers climb faster than my anxiety-addled brain can process.

"Fifty thousand from the gentleman in the back!"

"Sixty from the lady in red!"

"Seventy-five thousand!"

Holy fucking shit. My painting—created during lonely nights in my Queens studio—is generating serious collector interest.

"One hundred thousand!" calls Damon Wellington.

"One hundred twenty-five!" responds Sarah Chen.

The bidding war continues, each increase making my head spin. Then Xander's voice cuts through the competitive noise.

"Two hundred fifty thousand dollars."

The ballroom falls silent. That's more than double the previous bid, enough to make everyone turn and stare.

"Xander, what are you doing?" I whisper.

But he's not finished. He stands, every eye in the room focused on his commanding presence.

"Actually," he says, his voice carrying clearly through the elegant space, "let me be completely honest about why I'm bidding on this piece."

Oh God. Oh no. He's going full public declaration mode in front of Manhattan's entire social elite.

"This painting represents the moment I realized I was completely, desperately, irrevocably in love with the artist who created it." His ice-blue eyes find mine across the crowded room. "Not because she needs my financial support, but because she creates beauty that makes me understand why art matters more than money."

The collective intake of breath is audible.

"Rachel Brooks doesn't need my wealth to validate her talent. Her work speaks for itself, as tonight's bidding clearly demonstrates. But I need her creativity, her honesty, her incredible ability to transform vulnerability into strength."

He moves toward the stage where I'm standing frozen in shock.

"So yes, I'm bidding on this painting. Not only because I want to own it, but because I want to support the woman whose art taught me what love actually feels like."

The auction room erupts in appreciative murmurs. Several people start applauding, and suddenly the entire ballroom is clapping while Xander approaches me with obvious intent.

"Rachel Brooks," he says, dropping to one knee right there on the auction stage while hundreds of Manhattan's wealthiest watch, "will you marry me?"

Chapter 20
Xander

Holy fuck. Did I just propose to the woman I love in front of Manhattan's most influential collectors?

Yes. Yes, I absolutely did.

The ballroom holds its collective breath while my knee starts aching against the polished marble floor. Somewhere in the crowd, Gael's voice cuts through the silence like a blade.

"Jesus Christ, Xander! About fucking time!"

That breaks the spell. Laughter ripples through the audience, and suddenly Rachel's face transforms from panic to pure radiance.

"You magnificent bastard," she whispers, tears streaming down her cheeks. "You proposed at my first major auction?"

"I proposed when I couldn't stand another second without knowing you'd be mine forever," I correct, still kneeling like some medieval knight declaring fealty. "The timing just happened to be spectacularly public."

"Get up here and kiss her, you romantic fool!" Peyton shouts from somewhere near the back, her voice carrying clearly through the elegant space.

I stand, pulling the vintage emerald ring from my pocket—a 1920s piece that reminded me of her eyes the moment I saw it. "This was my grandmother's. She told me to save it for someone who made me believe in love instead of just compatibility."

Rachel's breath hitches as I slide it onto her trembling finger. "It's perfect. Like it was made for me."

"Everything about you was made for me," I murmur, then louder for our audience: "Is that a yes, sweetheart?"

"That's a hell yes, you presumptuous billionaire." She throws her arms around my neck, and when our lips meet, the ballroom erupts in thunderous applause.

The kiss tastes like champagne and forever, her mouth soft and desperate against mine. I lose myself in the vanilla scent of her hair, the way she fits perfectly in my arms, the knowledge that she's finally, officially mine.

"Get a fucking room!" Julian calls out, but his voice carries obvious joy.

I break the kiss reluctantly, grinning at my brother. "We will. But first, I believe someone was bidding on my fiancée's artwork."

The auctioneer, clearly experienced with dramatic interruptions, clears his throat professionally. "Do we have any additional bids beyond Mr. Ramsey's two hundred fifty thousand?"

Silence. Complete, respectful silence.

"Sold to Mr. Ramsey for two hundred and fifty thousand dollars!"

The gavel comes down with finality, and suddenly we're surrounded by well-wishers offering congratulations and business cards. Damon Wellington pumps my hand enthusiastically while Sarah Chen kisses Rachel's cheek with genuine warmth.

"Extraordinary evening," Damon declares. "The proposal, the artwork, the sheer romantic audacity of it all. You've given Manhattan something to talk about for months."

"Just what every girl dreams of," Rachel laughs, wiping tears from her cheeks. "Having her love life become society gossip."

"Better gossip than Hunter's vandalism campaign," Christina appears beside us, elegant as always. "Though I have to say, Xander's timing is impeccable. Nothing says 'serious relationship' like a quarter-million-dollar engagement ring and a public declaration of eternal devotion."

"Was it really that much?" Rachel asks, examining the vintage emerald with new appreciation.

"The ring or the painting bid?" Gael materializes with champagne flutes and his trademark smirk. "Because honestly, both were fucking expensive ways to get laid, even by your standards."

"Gael," I warn, but Rachel's laughing.

"He's not wrong. You could've proposed in private and saved yourself two hundred fifty grand."

"Where's the fun in that? Besides, now everyone knows you're off the market permanently." I pull her closer, possessive satisfaction flooding my system. "No more speculation about temporary fascination or gold-digging schemes."

"Speaking of schemes," Julian approaches with obvious pride and mild concern, "Lauren looked like she wanted to commit homicide when you went down on one knee. I'd suggest increased security for the next few weeks."

"Already arranged," I tell him. "Though honestly, what's she going to do now? Object to our engagement in the society pages?"

"Don't underestimate a woman scorned," Christina warns. "Especially one with trust fund resources and flexible morals."

Before anyone can elaborate on Lauren's potential revenge plots, the auction coordinator approaches with paperwork and congratulations.

"Mr. Ramsey, Ms. Brooks—or should I say, future Mrs. Ramsey—we need to finalize the sale documentation. Also, three additional collectors have expressed interest in Ms. Brooks' future work."

"See?" I murmur against Rachel's ear as she signs purchase agreements. "Your talent speaks for itself. The engagement just gave people permission to express their admiration publicly."

Two hours later, we're finally alone in my penthouse, the sounds of the city forty floors below us while we process the evening's events.

"I can't believe you bought my own painting," Rachel says, curled up against my side on the leather sectional. "What are you going to do with it?"

"Hang it in our bedroom so I can look at it every morning and remember the moment I realized I wanted to wake up next to you forever."

"Our bedroom?" She tilts her head to study my expression. "Are we moving in together officially?"

"We're getting married. I assumed cohabitation was implied in the vows." I stroke her hair, marveling at how right this feels. "Unless you want to keep your Queens apartment as an art studio?"

"Actually, that's not a terrible idea. A space that's completely mine, where I can create without worrying about getting paint on your expensive furniture."

"Our expensive furniture," I correct. "Everything I have becomes ours the moment you say 'I do.'"

Her smile turns wicked. "Everything?"

"Everything."

"Including that ridiculous wine collection you never drink?"

"Especially the wine collection. Though I'm hoping married life gives me more reasons to celebrate."

She straddles my lap suddenly, her silk gown riding up to reveal the lacy garter belt that's been driving me insane all evening. "Speaking of celebrating..."

"Christ, you're gorgeous." My hands find her thighs, stroking the sensitive skin above her stockings. "Have I mentioned how much I love this dress?"

THE BILLIONAIRE'S MISTAKEN VOW

"You can love it even more when you take it off me," she breathes, grinding against the erection that's been plaguing me since she accepted my proposal.

"Here? Now? We just got engaged in front of half of Manhattan."

"Exactly. Time to celebrate properly." Her fingers work at my bow tie with obvious intent. "I want my fiancé to fuck me like he means it."

"I always mean it with you," I growl, lifting her enough to unzip her gown. "But after tonight, I mean it forever."

The dress pools around her waist, revealing perfect breasts encased in midnight blue lace. I lower my head to trace patterns with my tongue, tasting salt and expensive perfume and pure Rachel.

"Xander," she gasps, her nails digging into my shoulders. "Please, I need—"

"What do you need, sweetheart?" I ask, switching attention to her other breast. "Tell me exactly what you want."

"You. Inside me. Making me forget everything except how perfect this feels."

"With pleasure."

I carry her to the bedroom, laying her gently on silk sheets while I strip out of my tuxedo with desperate efficiency. When I turn back to her, she's removed everything except the garter belt and stockings, spread across my bed like a fantasy come to life.

"Fuck, you're beautiful," I breathe, joining her on the mattress. "My gorgeous fiancée."

"I love hearing you say that," she admits, pulling my head down for a kiss that tastes like champagne and promises. "Your fiancée. Your future wife. Yours."

"Mine," I agree, sliding two fingers inside her slick heat. "All mine, forever."

Her back arches as I work her closer to climax, her soft moans driving me wild with need. But tonight isn't about quick satisfaction—it's about claiming and being claimed, about sealing promises with pleasure.

"I want to taste you," I tell her, kissing down her body until I reach the apex of her thighs. "Want to make you come apart with my mouth."

"Xander, please—oh God—"

I worship her with lips and tongue until she's writhing beneath me, desperate sounds spilling from her throat. When her climax hits, she cries out my name like a prayer, her body convulsing with pleasure.

Before she's fully recovered, I'm positioning myself between her thighs, sliding inside slowly, savoring every inch of connection.

"Perfect," I breathe, starting to move. "You feel absolutely perfect."

"So do you," she gasps, her legs wrapping around my waist. "Like you were made for me."

"I was made for you. Everything I am, everything I've built—it only matters because you're here to share it."

Our rhythm builds gradually, intensely, until we're both trembling on the edge of release. When she comes again, the sensation triggers my own climax, and I bury myself deep as we fall apart together.

Afterward, we lie tangled in satisfied exhaustion, her engagement ring catching light from the city below.

"No regrets?" I ask softly.

"About the public proposal or agreeing to marry you?"

"Either. Both."

She turns to face me, green eyes bright with happiness. "Zero regrets. Though next time you want to make grand romantic gestures, maybe warn me first?"

"Where's the fun in that?" I kiss her forehead gently. "Besides, spontaneous proposals seem to work for us."

Epilogue

I'm standing in my new studio—a converted warehouse space in Brooklyn that Xander bought and renovated specifically for my artistic chaos—staring at a pregnancy test that's about to change our entire fucking world.

Two pink lines. Clear as day, bold as my latest abstract series, undeniable as Xander's obsession with buying every piece I create.

"Holy shit," I whisper to the empty space, my voice echoing off exposed brick walls lined with canvases in various stages of completion. "Holy actual shit."

My phone buzzes with a text from Peyton: *Emergency maid of honor meeting tonight. Need your input on whether chartreuse bridesmaid dresses would traumatize wedding guests or just photographers.*

Right. Peyton's wedding to Issac — the graphic designer she met at my first solo exhibition who somehow finds her crude humor charming instead of terrifying. Their love story involves more inappropriate sexual commentary than should be legally allowed, but watching my best friend discover happiness makes my heart stupidly full.

Another buzz, this time from Christina: *Museum board approved the retrospective for next spring. Congratulations, darling - you're officially important enough for pretentious art critics to analyze your emotional journey.*

The retrospective. My first major museum show, featuring pieces from my foster care days through present married bliss. A year ago, I was terrified of people examining my vulnerability publicly. Now I understand that sharing authentic experience creates connection rather than judgment.

My studio door chimes as Xander arrives for our lunch date, looking devastatingly handsome in his perfectly tailored charcoal suit. Even after a year of marriage, seeing him walk into my creative space makes my pulse race like a horny teenager.

"How's my brilliant wife today?" he asks, wrapping his arms around me from behind as I hastily shove the pregnancy test into my paint box.

"Productive. Overwhelming. Life-changing," I reply, leaning into his warmth while trying to figure out how to drop this particular bombshell.

"Life-changing how? Did someone commission a piece for the Louvre?"

"Not exactly." I turn in his arms, studying his face. "How do you feel about expansion projects?"

"We just expanded your studio last month. Though if you need more space—"

"Not studio expansion. Family expansion."

His brow furrows adorably. "Family expansion? Are Peyton and Issac moving in? Because I love your best friend, but her commentary on our sex life is already excessive without—"

"Xander." I reach into my paint box, retrieving the test with hands that shake slightly. "I'm pregnant."

The words hang between us like brushstrokes on fresh canvas, bold and irreversible and beautiful.

His face cycles through approximately seventeen emotions before settling on pure, radiating joy. "Pregnant. You're pregnant. We're having a baby."

"We're having a baby," I confirm, watching his ice-blue eyes fill with tears I've never seen before.

"Christ, Rachel." He lifts me off my feet, spinning me around the studio while laughter bubbles from my throat. "We're going to be parents. I'm going to be a father."

"You're going to be an incredible father," I tell him when he sets me down, cupping his face with paint-stained hands. "This baby is going to be so fucking loved."

"The luckiest kid in Manhattan," he agrees, his voice rough with emotion. "Growing up surrounded by your art, watching you create beauty from nothing, learning that love means supporting each other's dreams."

"Speaking of dreams, how do you feel about converting the guest room into a nursery?"

"I feel like calling my contractor immediately and designing the most spectacular baby room ever created." His grin could power the entire city. "Art supplies, tiny easels, colorful everything—our kid's going to think the whole world is a creative playground."

"God, I love you," I breathe, kissing him with desperate affection.

"I love you too. Both of you now," he murmurs against my lips, his hand settling protectively over my still-flat stomach.

My phone explodes with notifications as word spreads through our friend group. Gael's response makes me snort with laughter: *Called it! Domestic bliss leads to reproductive success. I demand Godfather privileges and the right to teach this kid inappropriate betting strategies.*

Julian's message is characteristically emotional: *Congratulations to my favorite brother and sister-in-law. This baby will have the most incredible artistic genes and family support system imaginable.*

Even Christina sends elegant congratulations: *Darling, this child will grow up in a world where love and creativity are synonymous. How perfectly wonderful.*

Six months into pregnancy, I'm waddling around our penthouse like a paint-splattered whale, working on pieces for the museum retrospective while Xander hovers like an overprotective caveman.

"You shouldn't be stretching to reach that canvas," he frets, appearing with a step stool. "What if you fall? What if the baby—"

"The baby is fine. I'm fine. Stop treating me like I'm made of spun glass," I interrupt, accepting the stool because honestly, my balance is shit these days.

"You're carrying my child. I'm allowed to be protective."

"You're allowed to be concerned. This level of hovering borders on psychotic."

Peyton chooses that moment to burst through our front door like a foul-mouthed hurricane, her new husband trailing behind with obvious amusement.

"Jesus fucking Christ, you two are disgustingly domestic," she announces, settling onto our couch like she owns it. "Xander, stop vibrating with anxiety. Pregnant women have been creating art for centuries without exploding."

"She was stretching—"

"She was working, which is what artists do." Issac, bless his patient soul, hands Xander a beer. "Trust me, I've learned not to interfere when creative people are in the zone."

"Smart man," I tell him, applying final touches to a piece about transformation and growth. "How's married life treating you?"

"Like a beautiful disaster filled with inappropriate commentary and spectacular sex," Peyton answers for him. "Just how I like it."

"We're very happy," Issac translates with obvious affection.

Three months later, I'm holding our daughter—Sophia Grace Ramsey—while Xander stares at her tiny face like she's the most precious artwork ever created.

"She's perfect," he whispers, one finger tracing her impossibly small hand. "Look at those fingers. Future artist fingers."

THE BILLIONAIRE'S MISTAKEN VOW

"Future whatever-she-wants-to-be fingers," I correct, though my heart melts watching him fall completely apart over our baby.

"She's going to change everything," he muses.

"She already has," I reply, studying the way sunlight streams through our bedroom windows onto this perfect moment. "Everything's more beautiful now. More meaningful."

Our penthouse has transformed into something I never imagined possible—a home where business success and artistic passion coexist with domestic happiness. Xander's private office showcases my latest pieces alongside family photos, while my corner studio space overlooks Central Park where someday we'll teach Sophia about colors and creativity.

"What are you thinking about?" Xander asks, noticing my contemplative mood.

"How none of this was in my plan. Foster care, struggling artist, falling for a billionaire who collects my work—it's like someone else's fairy tale."

"Better than a fairy tale," he counters, shifting Sophia so I can rest against his shoulder. "Fairy tales are fantasy. This is real life, messier and more complicated and infinitely more satisfying."

"Even when I'm covered in paint and baby spit-up?"

"Especially then." He kisses my temple gently. "You create beauty from chaos, sweetheart. Our daughter's going to learn that art isn't just something you hang on walls—it's how you choose to live your life."

Looking at our reflection in the bedroom mirror—Xander cradling our daughter while I lean into his strength—I see the masterpiece we've created together. Not perfect, but real and honest and absolutely beautiful.

This is what forever looks like: messy and challenging and worth every terrifying, wonderful moment.

Sneak Peak
The Bachelorette's Billionaire

The Bachelorette's Billionaire

Sloane

The bass thrums through my chest like a defibrillator trying to restart my social life, and honestly? It isn't working. I clutch my champagne flute like a life preserver, watching my sister Aubrey command the dance floor with the kind of effortless grace that makes me wonder if we're actually related.

"Sloane!" Aubrey's maid of honor, a statuesque brunette whose name I've forgotten three introductions ago, materializes beside me with predatory glee. "You can't hide in the corner all night!"

"I'm not hiding," I protest, adjusting my blue-light glasses nervously. "I'm... observing. Anthropologically speaking, this is fascinating behavior."

She rolls her perfectly contoured eyes. "God, you're such a nerd. It's adorable, but tragic." Her gaze sweeps across the club's VIP section, landing on a man who looks like he's been carved from marble and dipped in sin. "See that guy? The one who looks like he could buy and sell souls before breakfast?"

My eyes follow hers to the elevated VIP area where a man sits with the kind of casual authority that makes kings weep with envy. He looks like Zeus has decided to moonlight as a Manhattan power broker—all sharp angles and devastating masculinity wrapped in a perfectly tailored suit. Dark hair falls across his forehead in controlled chaos that probably requires more maintenance than my entire beauty routine, and even from this distance, I can see the sharp cut of his jaw, the aristocratic slope of his nose, and cheekbones that could cut glass. His expensive suit molds to broad shoulders and what is clearly a body that worships at the altar of expensive personal trainers. He is the kind of beautiful that makes women forget their own names, lose their inhibitions, and probably their undergarments too. He looks dangerous—the kind of dangerous that makes smart women do spectacularly stupid things.

"What about him?" I ask, though my pulse has already started doing interpretive dance.

"Beckett Reed. Owns this place and half of Manhattan. Also rumored to be hung like a—"

"Jesus, Madison!" I nearly choke on my champagne.

"What? I'm just saying, he's exactly the kind of bad decision you need to make." Madison's smile turns wicked. "I dare you to go talk to him."

"Absolutely not." I shake my head so violently my glasses slip down my nose. "I don't do dangerous men. I do spreadsheets and Netflix documentaries about serial killers."

"Which is exactly why you need this," another bridesmaid chimes in, appearing like a well-dressed vulture. "When's the last time you got properly fucked, Sloane?"

Heat blazes across my cheeks. "That's none of your—"

"See? Too long." Madison grabs my arm with the determination of a woman on a mission. "Go. Talk to him. What's the worst that could happen?"

Famous last words. I should know better. I have a PhD in data analytics—I understand probability and risk assessment. But apparently, three glasses of champagne have turned my brain into optimistic mush.

"Fine," I hear myself say, which is clearly my survival instincts malfunctioning. "But if I die of embarrassment, I'm haunting all of you."

I make my way across the crowded club, weaving between gyrating bodies and trying not to trip over my own feet. The rope barrier around the VIP section looms ahead like the gates of hell, guarded by a bouncer who looks like he bench-presses motorcycles for fun.

Before I can lose my nerve entirely, I duck under the rope with all the grace of a drunk flamingo. The bouncer starts toward me, but a subtle gesture from the man in question—Beckett—stops him cold.

Up close, he is even more devastating. Storm-gray eyes assess me with the intensity of a predator sizing up prey, and when his mouth curves into a sardonic smile, I feel my knees consider mutiny.

"Lost, sunshine?" His voice is whiskey and smoke, the kind that makes sensible women forget their own names.

"I—no, I—" I fidget with my charm bracelet, the tiny data symbols clinking together like a nervous tambourine. "Actually, yes. Completely fucking lost."

His eyebrow arches with what might be amusement. "Interesting vocabulary for someone who looks like she teaches Sunday school."

"Shows what you know," I shoot back, some of my usual sarcasm breaking through the champagne haze. "I teach algorithms to worship efficiency, not Jesus."

"A data priestess. How deliciously nerdy." He leans back in his chair, studying me like I'm a particularly intriguing equation. "What brings you to my den of iniquity, priestess?"

"Your den of—oh, you own this place." Brilliant deduction, Sloane. Really showcasing that advanced degree. "Right. Well, my sister's getting married, and apparently, talking to dangerous strangers is a bachelorette party requirement now."

"Dangerous?" He looks genuinely entertained. "What gave me away?"

"The way you're sitting." I gesture vaguely, champagne making me bold. "Like you own everything you survey. Also, your suit probably costs more than my rent, and you have that whole 'I could ruin your life with a phone call' vibe going on."

"Perceptive." He stands, unfolding to his full height, and dear God, he is tall. "Though I prefer to think of myself as selectively ruthless."

"Oh, well, that's much better," I say, sarcasm dripping. "Really puts a girl at ease."

"You don't seem easily intimidated, sunshine." He moves closer, and I catch the scent of expensive cologne and something indefinably masculine. "Most people who accidentally wander into my space apologize and scurry away."

"I'm not most people."

"No," he murmurs, his gaze dropping to my mouth for a heartbeat before returning to my eyes. "You're definitely not."

The air between us crackles with tension so thick I could slice it with a butter knife. This is insane. I am insane. I don't flirt with men who look like they could bench press my car. I analyze data and eat takeout in my pajamas and watch BBC documentaries about the mating habits of penguins.

But here I am, drowning in storm-gray eyes and feeling things that definitely aren't appropriate for public consumption.

"So," I say, desperate to break the spell before I do something catastrophically stupid, "do you always lurk in VIP sections looking brooding and mysterious, or is this a special occasion?"

"Always," he says without missing a beat. "It's in my job description. Right between 'intimidate competitors' and 'make spreadsheet goddesses blush.'"

"I'm not blushing," I lie, knowing full well my face is probably glowing like a traffic light.

"Of course not." His smile is pure sin. "Would you like another drink, or are you planning to nurse that one all night?"

I look down at my glass, realizing I've been gripping it like a shield. "I should probably—"

And that's when disaster strikes.

A group of overzealous party-goers stumbles past our little bubble, and one of them—a guy in an aggressively ugly tie—knocks into me. Hard. My champagne flute goes flying, the golden liquid arcing through the air in slow motion before landing with spectacular precision across Beckett's pristine white shirt and expensive jacket.

The entire VIP section falls silent. Even the music seems to dim. I stand frozen, watching Dom Pérignon drip from his lapels onto the marble floor, probably ruining shoes that cost more than my student loans.

"Oh fuck," I whisper, then immediately clap a hand over my mouth. "I mean—I'm sorry—I didn't—"

Beckett looks down at his soaked shirt, then back at me, and for a terrifying moment, I wonder if this is how my obituary will start: *Local data analyst dies of embarrassment after assaulting billionaire with overpriced alcohol.*

The Bachelorette's Billionaire

Snowed In With My Billionaire Boss (December 2025)

with love and thanks

Me. Chloe.

T hank you for reading ***The Billionaire's Mistaken Vow.***

At any time love can surprise you and your life take an entirely different direction...

On a personal note, if you care to leave a kind word or stars as a review on The Billionaire's Mistaken Vow, it would mean the world to me. And it will help other readers find their next read.

You can go to Amazon Chloe Horne. While you are there click the +Follow for news on upcoming releases.

Chloe

Turn the lights low, the music up, and fall into a Chloe Horne romance.

Chloe Horne Amazon

Engaged To My Billionaire Boss

One Night With The Billionaire

The Billionaire's Second Chance

The Bachelorette's Billionaire

The Billionaire's Mistaken Vow

Snowed In With My Billionaire Boss (December 2025)

And Chloe?

I've been devouring romances forever. Growing up in the land of make-believe made me believe Happily Ever After is always just around the corner. And romance is everywhere when you open your eyes.

I like my leading men like my coffee, strong and rich. Protective Alpha Heroes willing to be more than just their bank account. Men who are both entertained and amused by real women. Men who are strong enough to be a little vulnerable.

I like my leading ladies smart, curvy, strong, and ready to take on the world. I like them to give as well as they get. I like them to know what they want - in their men. In their bed. In their life.

Together, they arrive at their own Happily Ever After.

My hope is that at the end of each book, you don't want to say goodbye.

Personally, I love to travel. If there is a palm tree there, I'm there. Mexico, Brazil, the Caribbean, Hawaii.

My other passion is music, all sorts of music from sweet to salty, from reggae to rock, from samba to salsa, from country to classics.

Drop a line hello@ChloeHorne.com

Made in the USA
Coppell, TX
17 November 2025

63438425R00108